MURDER
IN
STONEY LONESOME

ALSO BY MARTHA DIETZ

Rue de Navarin
Luceta

MURDER IN STONEY LONESOME

A Novel of International Intrigue

By

MARTHA DIETZ

ARPress
45 Dan Road Suite 5
Canton MA 02021

Hotline: 1(888) 821-0229
Fax: 1(508) 545-7580

Ordering Information:
Quantity sales. Special discounts are available on quantity purchases by corporations, associations, and others. For details, contact the publisher at the address above.

Printed in the United States of America.

ISBN-13:   Softcover   979-8-89356-761-8
                eBook   979-8-89356-762-5

Library of Congress Control Number: 2024914396

CHAPTER ONE

Being involved with murder was nothing new to Abigail Abbott. She had been writing mystery series for television and scripts for movies for years. Her protagonists had been involved in all sorts of murders and mayhem using all sorts of murder weapons and involved in all sorts of intriguing situations. But being personally involved with a murder investigation in Brown County, Indiana, was a first. It was a first for anywhere. Abby had moved into a newly constructed home located on a hilltop among very tall, very old trees only two weeks before. She was still exploring her new surroundings when she and her standard French Poodle, Pamfou, happened upon a body in the dense foliage some distance behind the new home she christened Purity Manor II. The body was still on her property.

The area where Abigail Abbott chose to build used to be called Stoney Lonesome, but that name and small community had disappeared years before the widow Abbott bought this large plot of land near Nashville, Indiana. Abby rather fancied the name and liked to tell her friends she now lived in Stoney Lonesome, Indiana. Stoney Lonesome seemed quite an appropriate place for Abby to reside since she lost her beloved husband. Andrew Anthony Abbott, the Award-winning Hollywood Producer/Director who was renowned for his mystery movies and television shows was, himself, mysteriously killed while he was making a film in Sapporo, Japan. Abby, the head writer on all of Andy's projects, had been called back to the States for an emergency meeting of WGA, the motion picture union, and was about to rejoin her husband when word came that he had been killed. By the time she arrived back in northern Japan, Andy's body had been cremated without legal permission. Abby was presented with a decorative Urn filled with, she was told, Andy's ashes. Very few details of the actual accident were forthcoming from Japanese officials. From others in the cast and crew Abby learned that Andy had gone to scout locations on an island off the northwestern coast of Japan and had not returned. Supposedly, partial wreckage and bodies had been found but no one she could find had identified those bodies or saw the remnants of the wreckage. The bodies of the two others, the Lighting Director and Head Cameraman, were also never found. Abby got in touch with their families and learned they had been given the same story she had been given. The bodies were all so mutilated and burned that cremation was the only possible thing that could be done and so, without permission, their ashes were put in urns and given to the families whose losses were as devastating to them as was the loss to Abigail. Explanations that they all got were that the plane crashed in either an attempt to land or take off; and the bodies of the pilot, the producer, and two members of his production staff, had been recovered and cremated. No one seemed to know or care where the crash took place. Case closed.

Try as she did to learn more, there were simply no more details available to learn. This wasn't exactly the closure Abby would have liked, but there didn't seem to be any other course of action she could take. Then there was the terrible loss she felt that weakened her resolve to search further. Overwhelmed with grief she flew back to Los Angeles, in a way relieved to put an end to this investigation. Andy had been her friend, lover, husband, co-worker, and constant companion since they met in college some thirty years ago. No matter how long she investigated or the investigators she hired investigated, no matter how long she pursued the cause of the accident, Andy was gone. Life must go on for Abby. She must go forward with her life. It was what Andy would have wanted for her. It was what Abby wanted for herself. After the strange feeling that Andy would suddenly come in the front door abated, she did just that.

Andy had been gone two years now. Almost two years. At times it seemed like only yesterday that they were having breakfast on the patio of their palatial home in a gated community in Bel Air, California. At other times it seemed so long ago. It was almost as if it was in another lifetime. Innately optimistic, Abby forced herself to lead a full, interesting and, at times, exciting life. While she thrived on enthusiasm and always did, there was emptiness in that forced enthusiasm. She knew the reason. There was no one to share that enthusiasm with every day. But that's how it is and how it is going to be. So get on with it, she often had to chide herself.

Before his untimely death, Andy and Abby planned a retirement home in Somewhere, New Mexico. Abby had no desire or need to continue on with a writing career in Hollywood so she dragged out the plans and had their Dream House built. They bought property in Somewhere long before Somewhere was anywhere. It was long before it became an erudite retirement community bordering on a golf course with a beautiful country club and swimming pool and before it became a bedroom community for Albuquerque. Abby was happy in Somewhere in the home she dubbed Purity Manor. Andy always liked to answer the telephone: "Purity Manor. Purity speaking." Hence the name she gave her New Mexico home.

Abby was always an outgoing, positive person who made friends easily. She made friends in Somewhere. And friends came from all over the world to spend time with her. Many of those friends were famous actors, producers, and writers. Primed by the headwaiter in the Country Club dining room when the widow Abbott made reservations, the room did a bang-up business. No telling who would be dining with her.

Often a house guest was her friend Katherine Hastings. She and Kat had grown up together in Bloomington, Indiana, and had kept in touch through the years. Kat had been divorced, remarried, and then widowed by the time Abby lost Andy Abbott. Kat, who had retired to St. Louis, came to Bel Air immediately when she learned of Andy's death. Abby could always depend on Kat to be there when she was needed. They felt they were soul mates who could read each other's thoughts, finish each other's sentences, or come up with a name when the other friend couldn't. Abby often said she lost nouns, but her verbs were still active. Kat said she remembered nouns, but her verbs were lazy. The two pals roamed the state of New Mexico together, taking in all the tourist sites, and enjoying the stark scenery and all the interesting Indian reservations. They often visited Albuquerque. Santa Fe was only an hour's drive from Somewhere. Abby drove longer than an hour getting to lunch with friends in North Hollywood and in much worse traffic. Abby and Kat always had fun together. But Kat also had some responsibilities in St. Louis and returned to her own home. The minute Abby sounded down and melancholy, Kat was back at the Albuquerque airport. She made the trip so often, she knew the names of some of the stewards and stewardesses on the planes. Kat never met anyone she didn't know or find interesting.

Abby still laughed about one trip she made back to St. Louis with Kat. They were standing at the gate of Southwest waiting for a boarding pass. As usual, they were early. Kat started up a conversation with a man with a white cane. He was also waiting for his boarding pass. They were kidding back and forth, and Kat finally said to him, "Since you can't see, I feel I should tell you that I look like Cindy Crawford." Kat was not very tall and rather plump but that had never bothered her. The very jovial man finally admitted that he was only partially blind. Without a pause, Kat said, "In that case, I look like Sophie Tucker."

The trip went smoothly and when they landed in St. Louis and were reaching for their overhead luggage, another man tapped Kat on the shoulder and asked, "Pardon me, but aren't you Cindy Crawford?" There was laughter down the aisle. Kat laughed the loudest. Kat said, "I guess you didn't hear the correction. That was amended to Sophie Tucker." There was more laughter as the passengers exited the cabin.

Abby led a rather full life in Somewhere, but she felt she didn't really belong in New Mexico. Among other things, she missed green grass, trees, and shrubs; she missed the fall colors; she even missed the changing seasons. After all, she was a product of the Midwest. Her Hoosier background kept drawing her back for visits. Andy, too, was a Hoosier, and they were both ardent fans of Indiana University, their alma mater. Especially basketball.

When time and geography coincided with the NCAA Final Four games in which IU was a contender and sometimes winner, Andy and Abby would attend to root for their Indiana Hoosiers.

Abby often went back home to visit her mother. Alice Allison still lived in Bloomington, although by now Alice had sold the homestead and moved into Woodfield, a wonderful independent retirement community for seniors. It was a beautiful campus, full of interesting people. They had apartments and cottages. Alice had an apartment and, like her daughter, made friends easily. She happily joined in the multitude of activities, outings, trips, and parties. Abby was delighted her mother was still enjoying life. Alice had been a widow for quite a few years. Abby's father, an attorney, died of a massive heart attack a week after his doctor told him he'd live to be an old man. George Allison was 57 when he died. Anyway, Abby felt her mother was safe in Woodfield. If something happened, there would be help immediately. Usually Abby was miles, even continents, away from Alice. Knowing Alice was in a safe place and still enjoying and taking part in life, was a comfort to Abby. Knowing Alice was a happy camper was also comforting.

On one visit to Indiana, Abby and her mother drove over to Nashville, a small arty community just a short drive from Bloomington. Over lunch of black bean soup and French bread in their favorite corner restaurant, Abby remarked that when she was young she always wanted to either live in Nashville or have a summer cottage there. Her mother shrugged, "You still can, can't you?"

That thought gnawed on Abby. After lunch and on a lark, they stopped by Bridwell Realty to ask about available real estate. Jayne Bridwell leafed through a notebook of pictures of different homes and cottages that were currently on the market. Abby wasn't impressed with any of them and said so. She also said that she would like to build on a larger piece of ground, one that had a scenic view. At that, the Realtor brightened and said she had just the spot. It was five acres of rolling ground but had a mesa-like flat area on top that would be a perfect setting for a home with a view from every angle. It was not far, she said, in an area that used to be called Stoney Lonesome. This property had been for sale for several years and the price had come down quite a bit. The realtor offered to drive Abby and her mother to see it. It sounded to Abby almost too perfect to be true. This ideal spot was off Highway 46 and quite a distance up a winding country lane. Jayne explained, as she drove, that a road would have to be paved, a well would have to be dug and a septic tank with a leaching field would have to be installed. Abby was familiar with all those necessities because she had them done in Somewhere.

Jayne parked the car in a partial clearing and said they would have to walk the rest of the way. The view was spectacular, and Abby decided then and there that Stoney Lonesome and this piece of property were meant for her. She was meant to come back home again to Indiana. The number one advantage was she would be close to her mother. She could even go to IU basketball and football games. How perfect was Stoney Lonesome. Besides, she loved the name. Stoney Lonesome. "It just rolls off the tongue," she said. In Abby's case it hit close to home. Lonesome, she was.

The deal was consummated. A house was designed by a local architect. The building was awarded to Hinkle Construction Company and Hinkle did his company proud. The result was indeed a beautiful structure, perfect in every way. Jimmy Lee Harrison, the architect, designed every room with a view. He fell in love with his own creation and offered to buy Purity Manor II at whatever price Abby named. Abby, too, had fallen in love with her Indiana home and refused all offers.

Abby and her longtime cook/housekeeper, Maggie Muldoone, the faithful house boy/chauffeur/foster son, John Wayne Wong, and Abby's constant companion, the big black poodle, Pamfou, moved from Somewhere to Stoney Lonesome. The move went smoothly, settling in went quickly and life was as near normal as Abby's life ever got.... until she and Pamfou came upon a dead body.

CHAPTER TWO

After word got out that a murder had taken place on the old Vonderschmidt property, all kinds of people invaded their privacy. Maggie insisted some of the people had no business there. They were merely rubbernecking. In such a small place, curiosity was widespread about the big house and spread that was being built on top of the hill. That property had finally sold to an "outsider" who had this mansion built.

Abby had been told that rumors ran amuck about what outsider built this rambling spread. Everybody from a Sheikh from Dubai with 4 of his wives to Magic Johnson and his family because he is going to buy the Pacers basketball team and he doesn't want to live right in Indianapolis. Others were sure it was an Emir from Kuwait because they saw a woman wearing a Burka covering her face. She was probably the Sultana of the Emir who bought that property. Others were afraid the Arabs were here to buy up our country.

Wong had seen people down the hill with binoculars. So had Abby who made a mental note to have a gate installed at the foot of the new driveway leading up to the house, a four-car garage, and a guest house.

Abby worked closely with the county sheriff, Abe Simpson. No one knew the name of the dead man and his fingertips had been mutilated so badly that fingerprints were impossible to obtain. It was curious indeed. Abby suggested the sheriff check with Jimmy Lee Harrison. Perhaps the dead man had been a member of his construction crew; or someone with the Septic Tank service that installed the tank and leach field; or one of the road crew. Nothing came of any of those leads. The dead man continued to be a mystery. The only thing certain about the man was that he was Asian, Japanese they surmised, and he had not been dead very long before Abby stumbled upon his body. The coroner, who also doubled as the local mortician, determined that the body had been dead for about two weeks, no more than three.

The spot where Abby found the body kept luring her back. Several times on her walks she stopped to search the area for a clue they might have missed. The man was not armed. His possessions were few, none revealing anything about who he was or where he came from or why he was there, or why he had been shot in the back of the head. It was on her third trip down to the murder scene that Pamfou, nosing around in the leaves, uncovered a slip of paper. On it was written Abby's name and address, only it was the old address in Bel Air. There was also a phone number. It was the unlisted number for the telephone she had in California.

Now Abby was really puzzled. Evidently this man came to find her. The why continued to nag at her. She expressed her curiosity aloud to Wong and Maggie. Wong said the man must have really wanted to find her because he obviously trailed her from Bel Air to Somewhere to Stoney Lonesome. Maggie warned her not to tell the sheriff what she had found or she would be involved.

"I'm already involved," she answered the housekeeper rather sharply. Then she dialed the sheriff's number.

Sheriff Simpson arrived two hours later at his usual casual pace with his usual unruffled demeanor. Abby wondered, now that she was more acquainted with the Law Enforcement Officer, if anything ever bothered Abe Simpson. She also wondered if Abe was a nickname for Abraham. Abe did resemble Abraham Lincoln. He was tall, lean and lank, dark haired with deep set eyes, and a rumpled look about him as if his uniform had never seen a dry cleaner. He was, however, clean shaven with close-cropped hair. Abby guessed that Abe was pushing fifty. Maybe even pulling it.

"How do you account for this?" he asked waving the slip of paper with the California address and phone number on it. "And where did you find it? We searched the area thoroughly where his body was found."

"It was buried under a pile of leaves at the foot of the Sycamore tree near where the body was discovered. Pamfou routed it out."

"That dog of yours seems to have an unusually keen nose. Why were you…"

"Yes," interrupted Abby not wanting to admit that curiosity kept bringing her back to the scene of the crime. "As for why he was hunting me -- or following me -- I can't explain. Can't imagine who he is or what he wanted. Obviously he didn't want a face to face confrontation or else he would have simply rung the doorbell. Those chimes can be heard all over the house. It couldn't be that we didn't hear him."

"The mystery is who didn't want him to find you? And why hadn't anyone here heard the shot? Your dog has a good nose. Probably has a good ear, too. And where were your servants?"

"I can't answer who didn't want him to find me. But the Coroner said the man had been dead two or three weeks. Perhaps he was shot before we moved in. We only arrived two weeks before. We arrived with the movers and while Maggie, Wong, and I were here to supervise the placement of furniture and unpack boxes, we didn't sleep here until the house was pretty much in order. We all stayed at the motel down the road."

"Hmmm. That's so. Well, you got me. You are assuming he was shot at night. Probably was. The shooter surprised him from behind. Easier done in the dark. Don't know what we can do about any of it now."

"I know one thing I can do," said a determined Abby. "I can telephone the people who bought our home in Bel Air. I can ask if anyone fitting his description came around asking for me. Or had there been anyone of any description asking for or about me."

"If you want to." The sheriff shrugged. "Let me know if you find out anything more." He picked up his well-worn ten-gallon hat and headed for the door. Wong beat him there and opened the ornate front door for him. The sheriff, accustomed to opening his own doors, only frowned. As an afterthought, he asked, "You Japanese?"

"Taiwanese. I'm from Taipei."

"You got any enemies?" asked the lawman.

"Not that I know about." Wong bristled. "I was an orphan when Mr. and Mrs. Abbott found me and brought me with them to America."

"Been here long?" Abe persisted.

"Twenty years. I was ten when they found me. I'm nearly thirty now. I've been with the Abbotts the whole time. They sent me to school and to UCLA where I graduated with honors."

"You're on the wrong track, Abe," Abby interjected. "I'm certain the dead man has nothing to do with Wong. Or Maggie. Or possibly not even me."

"Uh huh," he said doubtfully. The sheriff walked slowly to his patrol car that was sitting in the newly cemented parking area off to the right of the house and in front of the four-car garage. He wasn't convinced the murder had nothing to do with Abigail Abbott. Her Los Angeles address was a very convincing clue.

That night Abby awoke with a start. The bedside digital clock said it was 4:02 am. She had been having her now recurring bad dream. It was always the same. Andy was standing in the doorway of the Bel Air home they shared for so many years. He was smiling that mischievous little smile she loved and was so accustomed to, usually when he had played a trick on her and was waiting for her to discover what it was. Quite a jokester was Andrew Abbott. He always played pranks on the set to keep his actors loose and relaxed. In the dream, though, when she reached out for him, he disappeared. Then there was the hideous laugh that woke her up. It was always the same. Tonight was no exception although Abby seemed more unnerved than usual.

Not able to shrug off the sight and sound of her late husband, Abby got up and padded to the kitchen for a glass of milk and maybe one of Maggie's oatmeal cookies. To her surprise she found Wong at the window of the breakfast room peering through binoculars.

"Shhhh!" he whispered when she approached. "I saw a light bobbing among the trees. Then I thought I saw a shadow or some kind of movement. It seems to have disappeared now."

"What caused you to look for a bobbing light?" Did you hear a noise?" By this time Pamfou sensed some excitement and was beside them wagging and nudging.

"No, I didn't hear anything," Wong said. "I couldn't sleep and decided to patrol the house, maybe get something to eat. We have all these nightlights around so I didn't need to turn on any lights. When I opened the refrigerator, I thought I saw a light out of the corner of my eye. Like a flashlight. Not bright. Small. At first I thought I was seeing things, but after closer inspection I'm certain it was a light bobbing back toward the trees. Not my imagination."

"Maybe it was the refrigerator light reflecting out there."

"Maybe." Wong was not convinced but let it go. "What got you up?"

"Bad dream."

"Same old dream?"

"Yes. The same." Abby went to the refrigerator herself and pulled out a container of milk. Just then Pamfou barked and began clawing at the kitchen door.

"Ok," said Wong. "Settle down. You don't want to go out there. You might be attacked by a fox or a raccoon."

"Or that animal carrying a flashlight," Abby joked. "We'd have to get you shots if it bit you." To Wong she said, "I think this dead body business has got us all a bit rattled. Have some milk and cookies. Maybe we can get back to sleep and forget all about it."

If only it had been that simple. She couldn't get the bobbing light off her mind. By the next morning, Abby decided to call in reinforcements. When it was after eight o'clock California time, she dialed her friend and former CIA agent, Richard Anderson. There was no answer so she left a message on his voicemail.

CHAPTER THREE

Two days later Rick Anderson telephoned Abby from his Los Angeles office. "Sorry for my delayed response, Abby Dear, but I just got back in town and found your message. What can I do for you?"

"Oh, hello. Rick. Are you working on a new project?" Abby knew better than to ask Rick that, but it was just a conversational reaction.

He continued the conversation as if it was a natural thing to talk about his activities. Not mentioning the assignment he had just completed in Iran, he referred to the projects he and Abby did together. "Yes, and I sure could use you. Want to come out and doctor a script for me? It is in dire need of emergency surgery. Besides the mistakes they are making with intelligence details, the dialog stinks with a capital S."

"No, I don't want to come out there. But if you bring your sick script here, I'll see what I can do. Besides, I need you."

"Really? Need my what? Brains? Brawn? Incredibly good looks?"

"All of the above," laughed Abby. "I'd rather explain my predicament in person," she said in dead seriousness.

Sensing the seriousness in her voice," he said, "I'll be on the next plane. To where? Indianapolis?"

"Yes, Indy. I'll have Wong meet you. I'll come, too. It's Fall here and New England can't hold a candle to Brown County's Fall colors. This is an especially good year. You'll love the trip." A pause. Then she added, "Rick, thank you."

"Are you all right, Abby? You sound as if it is urgent."

"Might be. Might not be. I appreciate your help. And, of course, your friendship and support."

"And my brains, brawn, and incredibly good looks?"

"Those, too," she laughed.

"I'll get back to you with my ETA." Rick hung up the phone. Friendship. Yes, a long and lasting friendship. He would not have admitted it to a living soul, but he had been in love with Abigail Abbott since the day they met. It was on the set of Andy's second feature film. Rick had been hired to check on intelligence work details. After all, he had worked in intelligence, both Military and Federal, for a lot of years. In truth he still was, but no one knew that except the head of the Bureau. I guess you could say he was as under cover as one could get. His cover was retirement. Age and experience counted for something. Anyway, he always held his feelings for Abby in check and made no advances. She and Andy were so much in love it would have done him no good anyway. And it would have cost him the friendship of two people he really liked. When word got to him about Andy's death, he had been on assignment in the Middle East, stationed in the United Arab Emirates. He had visited Abby only once in New Mexico. There had been a house full of people so they had little time to talk. Rick looked forward to seeing her again but couldn't help wondering what problem was bothering her.

True to his word, Rick Anderson arrived at the Indianapolis airport the very next day and was met at the baggage carousel by Abigail. Wong drove around and around the airport while waiting for Abby and Rick to emerge out the doors. No one was allowed to idle on curbside while waiting for arriving passengers. On the ride back to Stoney Lonesome they chatted about everything except the reason Abigail wanted him there.

Wong took the scenic route back to Stoney Lonesome, and they all enjoyed the changing colors of the trees and shrubs in the beautiful hills of Brown County. As they drove up the newly built road and then the driveway leading to the house, Rick exclaimed, "Abby, how did you ever find this place? This view is spectacular, and the house is incredible. No wonder you don't want to buck the freeway traffic in LA."

"I have no interest in doing that without...." Her voice trailed off.

"I never did know the circumstances of Andy's death. In Japan, wasn't it? Plane crash?"

"Let's save that conversation for later," she said as she took his hand and led him in the front door being opened now by Maggie Muldoone.

"Maggie, my love!" Rick exclaimed as he swept the Irish lady off her feet and spun her around in his arms.

"Oh, you!" she sputtered, blushing and straightening her apron. "Dinner will be promptly at seven," she said as the others laughed at her embarrassment.

"What's for dinner?" asked the guest.

"Your favorite. Irish Stew with dumplings."

"Maggie, my girl, your food is worth the trip."

Wong got Rick settled in his guest quarters. He had been purposely put in the suite facing the woods in the back of the house. No matter. One guest suite was as comfortable as the next, and they all had magnificent views.

After drinks and dinner, Abby and Rick settled down in the cozy living room with their coffee and brandy. Dessert would have to wait. They had all eaten much too much. Wong, a self-proclaimed Computer Freak, had retired to his rooms to spend another evening on his computer. Maggie was busy cleaning up the kitchen, happy that her dinner had been a success. Rick had seconds of everything. That man needs a few good meals, Maggie thought to herself.

In the living room Rick said, "Now, Abby girl, what's going on with you?"

Abby told him in detail what had transpired so far. Getting the call from some Japanese official in Sapporo, going over and finding what little she could about the accident, and about the ashes in the urn, and how she was stonewalled by the Japanese officials. Rick listened intently, sometimes shaking his head in disbelief or maybe it was disgust. Then she told him about finding the body in the woods, the investigation that led nowhere, the autopsy that turned up nothing except death caused by a bullet to the back of the head, the mutilated fingertips, and then the note Pamfou dug up. She also told him about the light Wong thought he saw in the middle of the night. That's when she telephoned him. Rick paid close attention to all the details. After all, he was a detail-oriented person. He asked a question here and there but made no comment.

"Not much to go on," he said when Abby seemed out of conversation. "The bobbing light. That's interesting. Did Wong only see it once?"

"Yes. And he's looked every night since. That's why he insisted on putting you in that particular guest suite. It overlooks the woods where he saw, or thought he saw, the light."

"Could someone be mushroom hunting or ginseng hunting or some kind of hunting? I'm a city boy myself."

Abby shrugged. "I'm thinking of fencing the entire property with some sort of security fence. What do you think?"

"Not a bad idea. How big is the property?"

"Five acres."

"Ouch! That would be a costly project. Even if a security alarm was breached you would have too much area to cover. Why not just enclose and alarm the immediate area around the house and grounds?"

"Better idea. Oh, thanks, Rick, for coming. You were the first person I thought of to ask for help. I know I'm infringing."

"Nonsense. I'm glad you thought of me first," he said and took her hand and held it. They smiled at each other. Abby didn't miss the affection in Rick's eyes, but she wasn't ready for anything like that. Yet. She was barely fifty and it wasn't out of the question that she find another person to spend the rest of her life with. But not yet. It was too soon. She wasn't ready yet. In her heart she wasn't certain Andy was really dead. Just a feeling. Perhaps wishful thinking. However, should that day come, Rick would definitely be in the running. She really liked him, always had.

"It's been a long day. A long couple of months for me. I just got back from abroad when I listened to your message and called you. How about we sleep on it, take up where we left off in the morning. I'd like to explore the woods and the scene of the crime in daylight."

"Good idea. Would you like some dessert first? Maggie made your favorite, apple pie."

"Now how could I refuse Maggie's apple pie?" He got up and started toward the kitchen. "Maggie, my Luv, how's the chances of getting some of your apple pie?"

By the time Abby awoke the next morning, Rick, Wong, and Pamfou were already looking over the property. Thorough as he always was, Rick insisted on looking at all sides, not just the area in question. He wanted to know how many places of entry there were and if an entry was possible. On the north side there was a very sharp, deep drop with ravines here and there. No one would try to traverse that, especially at night, if there was another way. On the east side was the wooded area that led to a path that led to a farmhouse. That house looked unoccupied, but now was not the time to explore someone else's property. Then, of course, there was the west side up the newly paved road off route 46. That would be the path everybody took unless they were trespassing. The south side led to a corn field. Rick supposed anybody could come in there, but they would have to go around the back of the house to get to where the body was found. They could easily be seen. Unless it was dark. Then there was that bobbing light at four o'clock in the morning. He was amassing facts in his sharply investigative mind.

The day was beautiful, the air smelled of autumn, and the sky was blue and cloudless. All this made the chore a pleasant one. Rick was especially interested in the perimeter of Abby's spread, not just the scene of the crime. Wong, who had already cased Abby's property lines, was delighted to show Rick around. The two men talked amiably. Rick had known Wong since he was a boy and now enjoyed him as a man, albeit a young man, but with a good head on his shoulders.

Abby, in the meantime, had breakfast on the patio located through glass sliding doors in the formal dining room area. It was a lovely autumn morning and she wondered how many more days she would have before cold weather set in. As she remembered her formative years in Indiana, snow sometimes stayed on the ground for several days. She remembered her mother saying the winters weren't as harsh as they used to be in Indiana. Well, she thought, if it gets too bad, we can always pack up and go back to Somewhere. Or to Florida. Or to some warm place. A telephone bell interrupted her reverie.

"It's a good morning in Purity Manor," she answered cheerily.

"I'm just checking to see if you really get up as early as you say." It was the voice of Abby's lifelong best friend, Katherine Hastings, long since nicknamed Kat in grade school. Kat, a year older than Abby, graduated high school a year ahead of her and went off to New York to pursue a career while attending Columbia University. Kat had an older sister there who claimed she needed help with her young twin daughters. Kat lived with her sister and their family, helped with the chores, babysat, worked at a day job, and attended class in the evening. Back then that was more the norm for getting a college education than today with all the scholarship programs, financial aid, and parents' contributions. It was especially true for girls, determined to pursue a career that wasn't teaching, nursing or secretarial.

"Hey, what's your day going to be like?" asked Kat. She and Abby talked nearly every day. Once Abby's mother walked in while Abby was on the phone and she had said, "Say hello to Kat." After Abby hung up, she asked her mother, "How did you know I was talking to Kat?" Her mother replied, "You were laughing."

And that's how it was with Abby and Kat. They were more like sisters, sisters who loved each other as opposed to some sisters who were in constant sibling rivalry. Kat had a needy, quarrelsome sister like that. Abby and Kat had kept in touch and saw each other occasionally for many years. Abby was Kat's Maid of Honor at her first marriage to Raymond Hastings, with whom she had five children. Kat had said she had two of those children for Abby, so she need not bother with pregnancy. "Is that a friend or what?" Abby always said when telling the story of this enduring friendship.

Ray had walked out of that marriage leaving Kat to raise those five little children by herself. It was very difficult for her because she had no money, no job, nothing but a rented house and a cupboard with only bread, cereal and peanut butter on the shelves. Abby imagined how scary that must have been for Kat, who never admitted to fright or need. Abby and Andy were married by that time, themselves struggling to make ends meet in Los Angeles. Kat somehow made it through without asking for help and with an outrageous sense of humor about the whole thing. Possibly that sense of humor has gotten her through many crises in her life. When she finally told Abby of the divorce, Abby asked what happened. Kat replied, "He said my nose was too big and I was over-sexed." That was Kat.

The job she got to house, feed, clothe, and educate those children led to some very good things. She was a reporter and later a columnist for the Louisville Courier-Journal. Kat's column was syndicated in 329 newspapers and she was also in demand to talk to groups around the country and even in England. After the children were grown and through college, one was already in the Navy, Kat met and married Matthew Read. She never took his name legally because she was well-known as a columnist, speaker, and author. Abby met Matt only once and was out of the country when they were married. Somewhere in the years following, the friends lost track of each other. Kat was traveling and moving around the country; Abby and Andy were off to various out-of-the-way places making movies or television series. Mail was returned at both end, and it wasn't until after Matt's death that the girls got back together.

Having gotten Abby's telephone number from a mutual friend and former high school classmate, Kat's first words when she called Abby were: "As I was saying.....twenty years ago." It was as if they had talked only the day before. They took up their friendship where it had been interrupted and it had been like that ever since. Kat was always there and here she was again, calling just when Abby was thinking about her.

"Hey, I was sitting here on my Veranda...."

"Your Veranda? Are you wearing your bonnet and churning butter?"

Ignoring Kat's interruption, Abby continued. "I was thinking about where we should go when it gets cold and miserable here in the Midwest."

"Let's not go to Florida as we planned. The Keys can wait. Too many mosquitoes and bugs. Perhaps we should go back to New Mexico."

"Why New Mexico?" asked Abby. "I didn't know you were that happy there."

"I was happy there. You just couldn't tell by the frown on my face. It won't be full of Snowbirds, loud, raucous pool sitters, and over aged bleached blondes looking for husbands. Besides, it makes my feet ache when I watch them tottering around on those over-high heels in their pursuit of misery."

"You are probably right. Somewhere is still there and so is Purity Manor I. The house has a few less furnishings, but they can always be replaced."

"Oh, Goodie. We can shop." Kat loved to shop. Abby didn't. Kat perused every aisle and felt every item in a store. Abby went directly to whatever she was in the market for, found it, liked it, bought it. Then she would find a seat somewhere near and wait for Kat. Abby got a lot of thinking and/or writing done while waiting for Kat on their shopping sprees.

"We'll drive."

"You mean Wong will drive."

"Well, yes. We'll pick you up as we pass through St. Louis. Be standing along I-44 at the Kings Highway exit. Wong will slow down as you jump in the SUV."

"Ok. I'll be wearing my pretty peach outfit that will clash with my awful red luggage that nobody can lift. Not even John Wayne Wong. Hey, I want to spend some time in Santa Fe. There's a bunch of stuff I want to buy there. Did you get that article I cut out of the New Mexico Magazine?"

"I got it." said Abby. "We've already been to Chaco Canyon twice."

"I want to go again. And to Zion. And to the Four Corners. We never did do the Four Corners. Also we can visit my niece and sister-in-law in Durango." Kat was always so full of enthusiasm and raring to go. She was interested in everything including the tumbleweed that blew across the road and the Roadrunners perched atop adobe houses. "Inquiring minds want to know," she would say.

"I want to go back to Zion, too. There is so much beauty in New Mexico and Arizona. Stark beauty, but beauty." This was Abby chiming in.

Kat agreed. "Well, now we have something to look forward to. Any further news on the dead body?"

"No, but my friend, Rick Anderson, is here. He and Wong are out surveying the five acres now."

"The CIA guy? Calling in the big boys now. Good for you." Kat was truly worried about Abby.

"For advice mostly. Wong thought he saw a light bobbing about back there where the body was found."

"When was that?" Kat was alarmed. "You didn't mention that. That's scary."

"We weren't sure it wasn't just a reflection."

"Reflection from what? The stars? The moon? A satellite?"

"Our refrigerator light. We had both opened the door. I don't know. Wong was certain it was a flashlight. By the time I looked out it had disappeared. But the more I thought about it, the more I thought about calling Rick. So I did. He came the next day, bless him."

"Well, girlfriend, keep me posted. If you need me, I'm here. Or there. Or a lower case somewhere. Bye for now."

"I will. Thanks. Have a good one!"

"If I don't, I will take Milk of Magnesia."

Abby hung up the phone laughing.

She busied herself reading the Indianapolis Star newspaper. She had already worked the crossword puzzle and the Cryptoquip. Abby said she couldn't start the day without her Cryptoquip fix. That obsession started in New Mexico in the Albuquerque Journal. A good friend who lived across the road from Purity Manor I in Somewhere had gotten Abby hooked on the puzzle. She would start taking the Bloomington paper when IU basketball started. She was an avid basketball fan. Wherever she was, she followed the local basketball team. In LA it was the Lakers. In Somewhere it was the Denver Nuggets. Here she would follow the Pacers. When people were surprised that she was such a basketball nut, she explained that she was born in Indiana. Everyone born in Indiana got vaccinated with Naismith Serum in the Delivery Room. Dr. Naismith invented the game of basketball. A great invention even if he was in Kansas. Naismith serum causes Hoosier Hysteria, she would explain. Obviously that vaccination took on Abby. Andy joined her in following sports. She missed him for that. She missed him for a lot of things.

It was quite awhile before Wong and Rick walked up the long driveway with Pamfou leading the way. They were greeted by "Find anything interesting?"

"Maybe," said Rick as he put an arm around Abby who had walked down the drive to meet them. "Found some cigarette butts. Unusual brand. Might be Japanese. Since I don't smoke, I am not up on brand names. I'll find out though. And then we found this. He took a small pin from his pocket. "Looks like a lapel pin but the back is missing, just the pin part dropped out yonder. Could have been dropped by anybody, not necessarily the dead guy. It was almost buried in the mud but a corner glistened from the sun shining through the trees."

Abby took one look and swooned slightly in Rick's arm. "What is it?" he said holding her tighter. "Do you recognize it? Looks like a mask of some sort. It's pretty scarred up."

"It's Andy's Comedy Club pin. He was a member of the Hollywood Comedy Club. I recognize the comedy and tragedy masks. Looks like part of the tragedy has been broken off. But I know that's what it is. Or was." Rick helped her into the living room and sat down beside her on the long couch. She was visibly shaken.

"Now, my Girl, tell me again about the circumstances surrounding Andy's death. Wong seems to think something was not right about what happened and how it was handled in Sapporo. I want every detail."

Rick listened intently to what information Abby could provide. Wong had returned with coffee and added details throughout Abby's telling and re-telling of the events. When they stopped talking, Rick's only remark was, "Not much cooperation was there?"

They all sat quietly sipping their coffee and thinking their own thoughts. Finally Rick stood up and said, "Abby Girl, I am taking you out for lunch. I think we need a change of scene from these woods. No argument now. But first I have some telephoning to do." Rick, obviously accustomed to issuing orders, said, "Abby, get your shoes on. Wong, get to your computer and find out about the information we discussed. And also about the brand of cigarettes."

They both left to go on their appointed tasks. Abby sat fingering the pin.

CHAPTER FOUR

Abby and Rick were in the restaurant of the motel where Abby and company stayed while waiting for the moving van to arrive from New Mexico. Today they sat at a table next to the wall of windows overlooking a colorful panoramic view of the area. Rick sat facing the entrance, as was his custom. They were exchanging small talk when Rick suddenly asked Abby to change seats with him. This done, he explained that he saw someone he knew but didn't necessarily want to see just now.

"Who?" Abby asked. She knew better than to ask such questions of a federal agent on business, but Rick was no longer working for the CIA. He had retired from the Bureau two years ago, shortly after she had moved to New Mexico, or so it was announced. And who would he possibly know in Nashville, Indiana?

"A guy I used to know. Let's talk of innocuous things, in case he spies me." Too late, he had already been spotted.

"Well, if it isn't Richard Anderson. What in the world are you doing in this part of the world? Working on a case?" Oliver knew better, or should have known better, than to ask that in front of strangers, but the truth was that he was curious and more than a bit alarmed.

Rick stood up to shake hands. Abby wondered if it was not a move more to tower over this man than to be polite. "Hey, glad to see you, Ollie," Rick lied. "I'd like you to meet an old friend of mine, Abigail Allison. Abby this is Oliver Gutinov. We call him Ollie." He didn't necessarily want Oliver Gutinov to know Abby's last name, and for some reason her maiden name had stuck in his mind.

Abby smiled at the intruder and said, "Excuse the word old. I will." They shook hands.

Rick remained standing. He was not about to ask Oliver to join them and fortunately they were at a table for two. "I'm retired now, old boy. No longer doing casework of any kind. Sightseeing with my friend here. Do you blame me?"

"Are you staying in the hotel?" Oliver persisted.

"We are leaving soon. Have already seen most of the sights worth seeing around here." Rick avoided telling a lie that could be found out.

Abby thought this man breathed a small sigh of relief as he made his way quickly toward the restaurant entrance. "Was it something we said? Can't be the food. He left before he was even seated."

"He's up to no good. Never was." Rick watched him leave.

"A colleague? He didn't make any bones about you being with the Agency. I frankly didn't like his face. Weak chin. Evil eyes."

"An evil man and not too bright," was Rick's only comment. "Shall we have the buffet?" he asked, changing the subject. Abby got the point and they ate sparsely while talking of other things.

On the way out of the motel, Rick stopped at the desk and asked the number of Oliver Gutinov's room. He was told that Mr. Gutinov and friend had checked out a few minutes ago. "Sorry you missed him," the room clerk said sympathetically.

Me, too," said Rick as he steered Abby toward the front door. He stopped short and said to the desk clerk, "I thought he was staying a couple of weeks. Wonder why he left now."

The clerk answered, "He's already been here three weeks. He left no forwarding address."

"Well thanks. I'll catch up to him later. You have been very helpful."

"Strange", said Abby

"Interesting", said Rick

On the short drive home Rick told Abby a little about Oliver Gutinov. He had been a CIA agent gone bad. It was discovered that he worked both sides of the street feeding information, some vital, to the enemy. For reasons not available to Rick, this counterspy was never convicted nor had he ever served any jail time. Rick heard he had been deported back to his native country that Rick thought was Russia but turned out to be Poland. Most of the information Rick got was through the ever-active grapevine. Since he had never worked with Ollie and only saw him occasionally around Langley, he paid little attention to what happened to him. Until now.

Back in Purity Manor, Rick excused himself and joined Wong in the office/computer room. "What did you find out?" he asked.

"Not much. I did get the phone number you wanted in Indianapolis." Wong handed him a piece of paper. "On the other information I've drawn a blank. But I am still trying."

"Thanks. Maybe I can get better website information if I can get hold of someone at this number," he said waving the piece of paper Wong handed him. "In the meantime try the newspapers on or around the date of the accident. Appreciate it." Rick went to his own suite and made a telephone call.

A few minutes later he found Abby in the kitchen with Maggie. "Abby Dear, may I borrow a car tomorrow? I need to meet a guy for lunch in Indianapolis."

"Of course. You want Wong to drive you?"

"No, I'd better do this solo. But thanks." After a hesitation he said, "Want to take a walk?"

The two old friends walked toward the woods in the back of the house to explore the area around the tree where the body was found. "We found those cigarette butts back there. The shooter possibly left them while waiting for the kill. The victim was shot from behind, wasn't he? Up there? He could have been followed and was being observed from back here. I believe that's the easiest entry on this side of the property. Do you know anything about that farmhouse back there?" Abby didn't. She didn't even realize there was a farmhouse back there.

He proceeded on, marking a path as he went. Abby followed Rick back farther into the woods when suddenly there was a crashing noise off to the left. Someone fell from a tree. It was a boy, hardly in his teens. By the time Abby and Rick reached him, he was trying to get up. His leg appeared to be injured. Binoculars had fallen along side of him. Rick reached him first with Abby close behind. "What are you doing here? Casing the house?"

In pain and shaking with fright, the kid wailed, "I think I've broken my leg."

"I'll call 911." Abby said, turning back toward the clearing and the house.

"No! You can't. I don't have any money."

"Well, we can't leave you here. Where do you live? Can I call your parents?"

The injured intruder hesitated for a moment, then said, "I...I don't have parents. And I'm homeless."

"Why were you here casing this house?" Rick asked none too nicely.

"Some guy gave me twenty dollars and loaned me these eye things. He promised he would give me twenty more when I returned with information and these," he said, pointing to the binoculars.

"What information? Who was the guy?"

The kid was trying to get on his feet now. It was the left leg that was injured. If it wasn't broken, it was badly sprained. "Let us at least help you back to the house. We can talk there," Abby said helping him up. Rick, on the left, and Abby, on the right, held the brunt of his weight as he hopped clumsily on one foot.

Once inside, Maggie attended to the injury while Pamfou sniffed the newcomer. Pamfou got a snout full. The kid, whose name was Bobby Joe, was badly in need of a bath, shampoo, and some clean clothes. That would have to wait until Maggie finished her treatment. She cut away the dirty cloth from the injured leg. BJ, as he preferred to be called, looked horrified. Abby noticed and said, "Don't worry. We'll get you new jeans. A new shirt, too." As an afterthought and after surveying his condition, she added, "New shoes, too."

"But Lady, I already told you I don't have no money."

"Except that twenty dollar bill the man gave you with twenty more forthcoming."

"But I spent that twenty already on food for my Ma."

"I thought you didn't have parents," Abby countered.

"Ma is all I got and she's sick most of the time. She needs food or she ain't gonna get well. That's why I was doin'....what I was doin'."

"Where is your mother now? You said you haven't a home either. Where is she in bed?"

"Well, Ma'am, we're staying temporarily in an old shack back up in the hills. Guess we ain't supposed to be there. Come huntin' time we'll have to clear out. Don't know where we'll go."

"What exactly were you supposed to find out?" Rick had been staying in the background letting the women tend to the patient.

"If there was a man livin' here. He said I was to keep on lookin' until I saw a man and I was to describe him. How tall was he, how old, color of hair. That kind of thing."

"Then what?"

"I was to report to him this evening outside the courthouse."

"Does he work in the courthouse?"

"No. Well, I don't guess he does. I ain't never seen him before. He found me in the alley behind Mattie's. Sometimes they throw out some good food in the dumpster. I was looking to see if there was anything there."

By way of explanation, Abby said, "The courthouse is a common meeting place for people. They have benches outside where people meet, visit, and pass the time of day. Mattie's is a local restaurant."

"When did this happen?"

"When did what happen?" BJ was confused.

"When did this man find you?"

"This afternoon. Ma and me, we had nothing to eat since yesterday morning. Ma, she needs food bad. She's so sick."

"What did this man look like?" persisted Rick. "Short? Tall? Young? Old?"

"He was about my size, maybe a little taller. I'm big for my age. I'm fourteen. Kinda plump. Wore glasses. Had a moustache. Not much hair on his head and it was getting gray."

"Uhhuh," Rick said thoughtfully.

Maggie Muldoone cleansed the boy's leg and examined it. She had been a Nurses' Aide in her youth. Maggie proclaimed as far as she could tell the leg was not broken. She said BJ should soak in a hot tub and left to prepare the water. Abby guessed she'd be putting some Epsom Salts in the water to treat the sprain. Maggie was very big in soaking in Epsom Salts.

"I gotta get them things back to that man. I was to meet him no later than five o'clock this afternoon. You see, I need the money."

Rick said, "Tell you what, BJ, I'll collect that money for you. I'll return those binoculars myself. Here is your second twenty." Rick took a twenty dollar bill out of his wallet.

"But….but…. he needs the information."

"I'll give him the information in person. He wanted to know if a man was staying here. I'll let him see me in person."

"Okay," he said. "I guess." The leg still hurt.

Wong, who had joined the group along with Pamfou, helped get BJ into the sunken bathtub in the guest suite not occupied by Rick. BJ had never seen such a big bathtub with hot water and all, or such a big bedroom for that matter.

"Amazing what creature comforts we take for granted," mused Maggie mostly to herself as she left Wong to see to the bath.

"And how much we don't appreciate the things we are blessed with," added Abby. She left to talk with Rick who was cleaning off the field glasses, noting they were not of the best quality. "What are you going to do?" she asked.

"I'm going to return these, collect the kid's twenty dollars, and see who is interested in you and the man who may or may not be living here. Just paint me curious," he laughed.

"May I come with you?"

"Not this time. Much as I enjoy your company, you better stay here and tend to the boy. Knowing you and Maggie, you'll be taking food and tending to his sick mother, too. If he has one."

"You don't believe him?"

"Strangely enough I do believe him." Rick took the car keys from Abby and left the premises.

Rick stationed himself across the street from the courthouse. It was easily found with Abby's directions. Finding a parking space was not so easy. He finally parked behind a bank, walked through to cash a check, and proceeded out the front door. He busied himself looking at some original art pieces in the window of an art gallery. While feigning further interest, he stepped inside where he could see across the street and view both sides of the courthouse grounds. The old brick building was located on a corner facing two intersecting streets that, as far as Rick could see, had the only stop light in downtown Nashville. Promptly at five o'clock he saw Oliver Gutinov walk into the Courthouse yard. After their chance encounter at noon and BJ's description, Rick was not surprised to find Ollie behind this illegal business. It seems wherever Ollie was, there was some kind of illegal activity going on. Rick walked up to him, approaching from behind, and tapped the deposed Federal agent on the shoulder. "I'm returning these. I believe they are yours. Your messenger, or more accurately, your trespasser, is being detained. You owe him another twenty dollars, by the way.

Recovering from his surprise and making a bad mistake by glancing across the street at a big man emerging from an automobile parked illegally, Ollie stammered, "Oh…uh…I don't know what you are talking about, Rick. I'm just meeting a friend. Here he comes now." He started to leave but Rick held him back.

"What's going on, you son of a bitch? Why are you so interested in my friend and her house? Are you involved in the murder that was committed there a couple weeks ago?"

Rick noticed that Ollie paled and stammered some more. "Murder? What are you talking about?"

Mad as he was, Rick noticed Ollie hung onto the binoculars. "You know damned well what I'm talking about. If there is anything rotten going on, you're bound to be involved."

By this time the Incredible Hulk had come to Ollie's aid. "Trouble, Boss?"

"No trouble," Rick answered. "Your Boss and I are old friends. Isn't that right?" To the Hulk he said, "I'm just returning his binoculars."

"Ta for now, old Chap. We'll be in touch. Count on it." Rick said as he walked away. He thought it too much if he pressed for the kid's other twenty dollars, but he left Ollie clutching the binoculars. The two men stood staring after him, their mouths agape. Rick was pleased with the effect he had had on them. He went through an alley to his car in the bank parking lot and discreetly followed Ollie and the Hulk to Bloomington and to a motel on North Walnut Street. He noticed they went straight to a room so they were already registered. He watched them walk to Denny's restaurant and pondered whether to stay or go back to Stoney Lonesome. He waited awhile until he saw them amble back to the motel, go to their room and not come out, he decided they were merely underlings waiting for further instructions, so he headed back to Stoney Lonesome.

On the way home Rick wondered what they were up to and who was issuing the orders and why they were so interested in Abigail Abbott. It began to look like there was a connection between Andy's mysterious and unexplained death. Or was it just a disappearance? Too many clues were popping up: the dead Japanese person without identification or fingerprints, Abby's old Bel Air address and phone number, the mutilated Hollywood Comedy Club pin, and now the interest by a discredited former CIA agent with ties to Russia or maybe Poland. He intended to leave no rock unearthed no matter what barnacles were uncovered. He was just as certain that Oliver Gutinov was somehow involved. In addition to the bungled surveillance of Abigail, it was a gut feeling Rick had about that man. If he was a betting man, he would put a hefty wager on Gutinov's involvement.

Too many unexplained things, too many inconsistencies, too many discrepancies, and too many dead clues to be coincidences. Clues so long dormant had a way of disappearing, but Rick's bulldog tendencies would keep him on the case until he uncovered the truth. After all, Abby's safety, perhaps her life, was at stake. Seeing her again had stirred old feelings and old sensations in Rick. These must be suppressed awhile longer, until he got to the bottom of this. Tomorrow would be a good start.

Maybe.

While Rick was out chasing hunches, Abby and Wong, following BJ's instructions, made their way to the hunting shack. Inside there was a very sick lady shivering in a make-shift bunk. She had only a little throw rug over her frail body, and it was not keeping her warm. Startled when they approached, the woman drew back as if she was going to be hit. Abby said that they had come to take her to a warm place and get her well. She mentioned that BJ told them where to find her. The woman rebelled at first, but Abby prevailed and, weak as she was, the ailing woman allowed them to help her back to their car. Either she was too sick to fight back or the warmth in Abby's voice convinced her to cooperate. Or a little of both.

Maggie called a doctor they had met at a CVS store. She explained the situation and he agreed to make a house call. He was probably anxious to see the new mansion on the hill anyway. There are some advantages to living in a small community. By the time Abby, Wong, and the woman whose name was Hilda, got to Purity Manor II, the doctor was waiting there with his little black bag. He had already determined BJ's leg wasn't broken, just badly bruised. It had already started to discolor; and the ice bag Maggie put on it helped quell the swelling. After his examination, he said Hildy was suffering from pneumonia, dehydration, and probably starvation. He prescribed some medicines and went to the pharmacy himself to get the meds. In the meantime, Abby found some fleece pajamas and she and Maggie got Hilda into bed. BJ stood by her bed thinking he was going to wake up from a wonderful dream. Nobody had ever been nice to him, not in his whole life. His father, a mean alcoholic, had left his mother when Bobby Joe was ten years old. His mother was a waitress at the restaurant in the nearby State Park until their automobile broke down and she couldn't get to work anymore. They were evicted from their rental home because she couldn't pay the rent. One bad thing led to another and then they were out on the streets. Bobby Joe had to quit school because he didn't have a home address, wasn't vaccinated, and didn't know how to get help. After getting Hilda back to Purity Manor, Wong went to the store and bought new clothes for BJ. Once again, another dream from which he did not awaken. He offered the twenty-dollar bill Rick had given him, but Wong refused it, saying they were the ones who ruined his old ones. All this was really happening. Bobby Joe would sleep in the bedroom next to his mother's room. And they were both fed. He had never eaten such good food. And it was hot. Hilda got Maggie's homemade chicken noodle soup and an Ensure to drink. All was peaceful when Rick got back from Bloomington.

Peaceful for the moment.

CHAPTER FIVE

Rick was in Bloomington at 5:00 am the next morning. Sure enough Oliver's automobile was still in the same parking space. Thirty-five minutes later Ollie and the Hulk walked toward the car with their luggage. Driving a different car and wearing an IU cap and jacket he borrowed from Wong, Rick discreetly followed them to Indianapolis. They first drove through the drive-through at McDonalds while he parked in the lot in the AAA office next to the Fast-Food Emporium and when they left remained behind at a safe distance. In the State Capital they parked in an underground parking area beneath Washington and Illinois streets. Rick followed them up to daylight and across the street into The Conrad Hotel. He stationed himself off the lobby because the two men in question sat in the main lobby, obviously waiting for someone. Rick waited out of sight. Shortly after he had arranged himself on a sofa with a newspaper, he noticed someone else was interested in those two. When the other onlooker turned around, Rick recognized him as a fellow agent from LA. Rick sidled over to him and said, "Interested in Ollie, too?"

"Rick Anderson. What a surprise?"

"Walter Donnlevy. This is a surprise. I hope we are interested in the same guy and for the same reason. When were you promoted to Indianapolis?" The two men, who had been friends for years, clasped each other on the back.

"I'm not here. I'm still in LA. I've followed the trail of someone that led me here. Why are you here?"

"I'm just helping a friend out with a mystery. Seems her husband has mysteriously disappeared.

"Andrew Abbott? I remember you were close to the Abbotts in Hollywood."

"Why, yes. Is that what you are working on, too? Look, they're meeting someone. I don't recognize him. Do you?"

"Yes, I do. That's who I'm following. He's a scientist from Russia. We've had him in our radar for several years now. He is a scientist who is developing different viruses, some deadly. We want to find out where he is doing this and who he is doing it for. What in the world is he doing in Indianapolis?"

"They're going in the restaurant now. Shall we?"

"No. He knows me. Or knows I am CIA. His name is Alexandria Bulswicki. He taught at a University in St. Petersburg but was fired for being such an extreme radical. You must be really radical to be described as radical there. Now he runs an experimental laboratory of his own on some island off northern Japan. He claims to have discovered a cure for every ailment known to man. He's psychotic, egotistic, an outrageous liar, cruel, divisive, vindictive, demented, and devious. The man has not one saving grace."

"Outside of that, he is a nice man?"

"The worst. So far we have found horrible things he has done to and for humanity, but we don't have any proof that he did them. He keeps himself out of the danger zone. We have raided his laboratory in Seattle, but he is never there. The latest word we got is that he moved his laboratory to some island in the Sea of Japan, but we don't know where it is located. We got word that he has something new, and evidently big, going down. I'm still with the LA office and have been assigned to follow him, find out what he is up to. Still can't figure out what he is doing in Indianapolis."

"Isn't Eli Lilly here?" asked Rick. If he is a scientist making pharmaceuticals ...."

"If he has contacted them since he's been here it is by phone or face time, or text. He could have done that from afar. He didn't need to come all the way here. I've had him in my telescope since he arrived two days ago. He is checked in here, by the way. What brings you here?"

"Oliver Gutinov."

"Oh, he's small potatoes."

"I know, but he has been casing Abigail Abbott's house down in Brown County. They found a dead Japanese man in her back yard. No ID. Fingertips so mutilated there was no identifying him. There was a note found on him with her and Andy's Bel Air address and phone number on it. She sold that property shortly after she was informed of Andy's death. Japanese officials in Sapporo told her he was killed in a plane crash, cremated and pieces of the plane were burned and disposed of, and she was given an urn full of ashes. From Bel Air she went to Somewhere, New Mexico. Then because her mother lives in Bloomington and Abby grew up there and was educated there, she decided to move back to Indiana. Evidently this Asian man, who was shot in the back of the head by the way, trailed her to all those places. One other clue we found was a piece of a Hollywood Comedy Club pin Andy wore. Since we've been friends for a long time, she called me for help. I got here two days ago. The night before I arrived her houseboy saw a flashlight bobbing about in the woods behind her house. Then I bumped into Ollie at a local restaurant down there. He seemed alarmed to see me. Later that day we found a boy Ollie had hired to case Abby's house to see if a man was living there. I assumed he was looking for me."

Walter was listening intently to Rick's explanation for his intervention in this case. "Don't be too sure. We have word, very iffy word, that Andy Abbott is still alive, was imprisoned by Bulswiki, we can't imagine why, and he has escaped and is running for his life. We've had no proof up to now, although this reaching out to his wife is very interesting. We didn't know she had moved to Indiana. Last we heard she was in New Mexico. But this sounds hopeful, maybe even possible. Do you think Bulswiki is in Indiana because he suspects Andy will try to join her? If so, that would explain why he is here and using such reprobates as Oliver Gutinov, another Russian, to track him down."

Word of Andy's possible escape hit Rick square in the pit of the stomach. If true, he was glad for Andy and for Abby, but that put a damper on his feelings for Abby. Again. Still….they could both be in terrible danger. Best he was here to help protect her and Andy, if he showed up, but Rick didn't know if he should tell Abby about this unsubstantiated news. She would get her hopes up, then if Andy didn't materialize or got killed trying to escape, she would suffer his loss all over again. On the other hand if she was in danger, she should know it. A quandary.

"How can I help you, Walt? What should I do? Should I go out and try to locate Andy, wherever he is, or stay with Abby and hope he finds her?"

"I don't know. I'll have to get back to you on that. I was told not to trust anyone at the Agency here even if I needed backup. Let me continue to dog Bulswiki. I can't imagine what his next move will be. You can be my backup. We'll keep in touch. For now go back to her place in ... what did you call it?... Stoney Lonesome?" They exchanged numbers and text numbers, shook hands, and Rick went back to Purity Manor II. He skipped lunch with the not-to-be-trusted local CIA agent. Fortunately he had run into Walt and gotten that information first.

On the drive back to Stoney Lonesome he decided to tell Abigail. Hopefully he could impress on her that the information was iffy, very iffy. She should not get her hopes up too high. It could be quite a fall if it were not the truth. Truth seems distant and very insecure at this point. Still, it is a lead, something that has been in very short supply.

"I knew it. I knew it. I knew it." Abby exclaimed when Rick told her what he had found out from his agent friend, Walter Donnlevy. "I've had the feeling all along that Andy was not dead. I felt it, Rick. I did."

"I know," said Rick. "But we shouldn't get our hopes up until we see how this is all going to play out. Walt is following the scientist who he and the agency think kidnapped Rick and his two companions. He is keeping me informed."

"What can we…shall we do?" asked a somewhat excited Abigail Abbott.

"We can go about our lives normally. Act as if nothing has changed here. They may have others watching to see if Andy shows up here. Do you have any fire arms on the premises?"

"Only a handgun Andy gave me for protection years ago. It's probably rusty by now. Wong has a shotgun he was going to use to go hunting with some pals, but after one hunting trip, he gave that up. Too compassionate. Mom has Dad's rifles and pistols stored away somewhere in Bloomington."

"Good. Let's go pay Alice a visit. That would seem a natural thing to do." Now Rick had a plan. "How are your house guests doing, by the way?"

"Wong has taken BJ under his wing. Teaching him how to use a computer. Actually giving him lessons on line and giving him a book to read. The kid seems smart enough. He's just never had a chance in life."

"Ouch. Me thinks we have another adoption coming on. How about the Mother?"

"She's doing much better. Maggie's number one goal is getting her well and strong enough to begin enjoying life."

"I doubt that she's ever enjoyed life. She seems beaten down. BJ is her only accomplishment, and she feels guilty not being able to care for him as she should. Mother guilt." Rick already had her number.

"Well, they can stay here until we get them both back on their feet. The doctor seems to enjoy coming back to see her. I think it may be Maggie's chocolate brownies. However, the young doctor is quite attentive to Hilda. Hilda is very pretty. And the doctor is unattached."

"OK, matchmaker."

"Yes, let's get back to my own matchmaking. If you want, we can go to Bloomington tomorrow to see Mom and get the guns. Can we get bullets? I know Dad never kept bullets, only the pistol he kept by the bedside had bullets in it. He kept it locked in the bureau by his side of the bed."

"Yes, let's do that. And now beddy-bye time. We'll mark tomorrow as Day one of the inquest."

"Inquest?"

"Project. "

"Should we let Sheriff Simpson in on it?" asked Abby.

"Not just yet. Good night, Luv." Rick hugged her.

CHAPTER SIX

Walter Donnlevy stayed on Alexandria Bulswiki's trail. He noted to Rick that the two he was following met Bulswiki every day in the lobby of The Conrad. Interesting, if not surprising, Walt followed the scientist to the CIA offices in Indy. That's why he was warned not to contact anyone at the local branch. Bulswiki stayed in the building for twenty minutes then went back to The Conrad. Walt decided to wear a disguise so he could get nearer to him. Not much else to report.

Abby and Rick drove over to Bloomington and took Alice out to lunch at her favorite restaurant, Bob Evans. They sat in a corner out of ear shot of other guests and explained what had happened so far. Rick bought Alice a loaf of Banana Nut Bread, for the road, he said. He had known Alice for almost as long as he had known Abby and Andy. She gave them the key to the Storage Unit she rented on Winslow Farm Road, and they dropped her off at the local Simon Mall. She said she needed to do some shopping and she would call Woodfield to come pick her up. She had to get back to Woodfield because it was Friday and she didn't want to miss Social Hour. It was always fun and she joined a group of ladies for wine, laughing, and dining.

"Alice has found out how to enjoy herself while growing old," remarked Rick.

He and Abby proceeded to the storage place, picked up the case containing the guns, and relocked the unit door. It was then that Rick saw Oliver Gutinov's beady eyes peering over the steering wheel of a car parked outside the entrance of the storage facility. He didn't mention it to Abby but purposely drove out that entrance and waved at Oliver. He noticed they followed them back to Stoney Lonesome.

"Shall we invite them in for a drink?" asked Abby.

"I didn't know you knew we were being followed."

"I've written enough scenes to recognize a tail when I see one," answered Abby, rather proud of herself. "Then they can see there is no Andy here. Maybe they'll leave us alone."

"I doubt it. But hey, it's worth a try." Rick proceeded toward the car down at the entrance from the highway, but it drove off before he could signal to them. Life went on for several days without seeing any intruders or anybody observing their compound. Three days after their Bloomington excursion, Rick went with Abby to the grocery store just to observe if someone seemed interested in their movements. He could detect no interest in their activities.

When they got back to the house, Hilda was sitting up in the den watching TV. She had on one of Abby's nightgowns and pretty robes. Maggie decided she'd feel better if she looked better. The doctor said she should move about and exercise her lungs as well as her body. Hilda did look better. BJ was laying face down reading the book Wong gave him. It was "The Adventures of Huckleberry Finn" by Mark Twain. Wong was nowhere to be seen, and Maggie was in her kitchen concocting the evening meal. Before they could take their coats off, the doorbell rang. It was the doctor coming to check on his patients. Abby went to check with Maggie, then came back and invited the doctor to have dinner with them. He gladly accepted. Rick smiled at Abby.

The evening went well. They had a delicious dinner of Swiss steak with potatoes and carrots and a Caesar salad, dessert of Cherry pie ala mode. They all worked a jigsaw puzzle on the dining room table. Maggie provided snacks and hot chocolate. Hilda said she felt much better and they should leave. They had imposed long enough. When asked where she would go, she had no answer.

"Right," said Abby. "You both will be staying here with us until we get you well and find you a job and a place to live. No argument now. We all enjoy having you here with us, don't we gang?" There was a chorus of agreement. The good-looking doctor's voice was the loudest. BJ smiled and Hilda cried. Nobody had given them help, understanding, and a roof over their heads. Not until now. None of them realized how exciting the next few weeks were going to be.

Abby was awakened from a deep sleep by noises she heard coming from below. She looked out her window but could see nothing but an empty drive and parking area. No cars. No people. Some noise. People yelling. It was a woman's voice and a man shouting back. She could see no one. Donning her robe and slipping into slippers she went downstairs to find Rick with his arm against the throat of a woman Abby didn't recognize. "What's going on?"

"I found this woman hiding behind the glider on the patio. She says she has a message for you." Rick let up his pressure on her throat. "Well, here she is. Give her your message."

"I was to tell you and no one else. It's a message from your husband. Are you Abigail Abbott?"

"I am. Where did you get the message and who gave it to you?" Abby was doubtful or at least cautious. Certainly hopeful.

Rick chimed in. "This may be a set up. Be careful, Abby."

"I am being careful. You may give me the message in front of this gentleman. He's family."

"Some gentleman he is," the unknown woman snarled. "I am only doing a good deed for someone I only just met. He asked me to tell you that he is alive. Of course he's alive. I was talking to him, wasn't I?" The woman had a cockney accent and she didn't look too clean or well kept.

"I'm sorry. It is only natural that we be concerned when we find someone lurking about the property. Please give me the message and tell me where you were talking to my husband." This was Abby trying to calm the situation. She really wanted to hear the message and find out where Andy might be hiding.

"I was sleeping behind a filling station on Winslow Road and South Walnut Street in Bloomington. He was inside looking through a telephone book. He heard me ask the man on duty if he knew anyone going to Nashville. I needed a ride and had no money. The woman paused to get her breath. He pulled me aside and said he would give me taxi money to Nashville if I would deliver a message to you."

Abby asked again, "What was the message?"

"It was Gloriana Frangipana." She stumbled over the pronunciation. "He said you'd know where that was. Or what that meant."

"That sounds like him." She had purposely not mentioned his name. Neither had the woman so Abby guessed Andy hadn't told her his name.

"I had to persuade the taxi driver to bring me all the way over here. I told him my son was very ill and I had to get there to take care of him. He felt sorry for me, I guess. Can I go now? Please."

"Not until you have had something to eat." By this time Maggie and Wong had entered the living room."

"Of course you can go. But where will you go? Where is your son? Is he here in Nashville?"

"Yes he is, but I heard there was plenty of food in dumpsters here in Nashville. I was living on the streets in Bloomington. Slim pickins there."

Maggie jumped into action. "Come with me, Dear. We'll get you some food you don't have to dig for." She led the woman who said her name was Fanny to the kitchen. Wong followed. Pamfou stayed.

"What do you make of that?" Rick asked. "I believe she is telling the truth. If he knows where you are, why didn't he come himself?" Rick was trying to figure out Andy's actions. "And I wonder how he found out you were here and not in LA or New Mexico."

"At least we know he is in Indiana." Abby said hopefully.

"And if he knows he must know that the people hunting him must know, too. He's staying away from you to keep you safe. And himself safe. What do you think the message meant? Strange words."

"It's a clue. I know where he is." Abby was excited.

"Where?"

"On the IU campus."

"It's a big campus."

"Yes, but I know, or think I know, the spot. It's where we had our first kiss. In the gazebo. Oh, Rick, we need to get over there."

"What do those words mean?"

"It's an IU thing." She was jumping around the room with joy.

"Wait a minute. Calm down. We are under surveillance ourselves. We don't want to lead them to Andy. Give me some idea where and how we will find this gazebo. I need to figure out a way to get there undetected and decide where we can stash him until we can get the mad scientist arrested."

"Arrested for what? Kidnapping?"

"Walt said he was doing heinous and horrible things to people. Andy can probably tell us what those things are and let the CIA take it from there. We can't bring him here and we can't put him in a hotel or motel where we can't protect him."

"Doesn't the CIA have safe houses?"

"Yes, but they aren't always safe. I want to make sure he's protected. We'll think of something." Rick didn't want to mention that Walt Donnelly was told not to trust the CIA in Indy because they think someone there is suspect.

"Somewhere," Abby corrected.

"No, they already know about Somewhere and probably have your place staked out."

"Not Somewhere, New Mexico. Hide him some place, somewhere," Abby was serious. Rick grinned. Seeing Rick's grin made Abby grin, too. He was kidding.

They both remained silent for a spell. Suddenly Abby jumped up and said, "I know the place. Woodfield Retirement Campus. In my mother's apartment. They would never think of an Old Folks Home, would they?"

"Did they follow us that day we picked up the weapons?"

"Yes. Remember, Oliver was parked outside the Storage Company. You waved at him"

"I wonder if they followed us when we picked up your mother. We didn't take her home. We dropped her at the Mall. She said she'd call for a pick-up when she was finished shopping. I was earnestly watching to see if we were being followed coming over. I don't believe we were, but…"

"That doesn't mean we weren't." Abby finished Rick's sentence.

"What sort of an apartment does she have? I don't dare try to see it. That would be a good place if they haven't already found out she is your mother. Only Oliver knows your maiden name if he even paid attention. He may not have been wise to the whole situation. He hadn't seen Alexander Bulswicki yet. What name is she registered under? How big is her apartment? Who would we have to let in on his presence there?"

"One question at a time, please. She is registered under her own name, Alice L. Allison. She has a double apartment on the third floor. It has two bedrooms and two baths, one at either end of the unit. A kitchen, a dining room, and a living room in the middle. There are two porticos, one enclosed and one screened-in. Chances are he wouldn't be roaming around the building anyway. She can bring his meals to him, or they can cook. Andy is a good cook, better than I am. Or we could lend them Maggie." Abby laughed. She continued, "They would deliver the meal, but for them to deliver meals for two, they would have to register Andy. With the gossip machine over there, a new man in the building would be great news. They would be besieged by widows anxious to meet a new guy, especially one as distinguished looking as Andy, and they would probably be receiving casseroles and cookies by the dozens."

"Hey, there's your food problem solved." Rick interjected.

"Only Andy doesn't like casseroles."

"Let me think about this for awhile. Would Alice agree to such a thing?"

"Of course she would. She loved — loves Andy. Plus it will improve her reputation if word got out that she was living with a younger man." They both laughed.

"One more question. Does she have neighbors dropping in on her without notice?"

"No. She once said she liked it there because nobody comes knocking on your door without first calling. Except Maintenance and Housekeeping. They knock, but they both have appointments so you would be expecting them at their appointed times."

"What about an escape route?" This was Rick still analyzing the situation.

"She has two doors in her apartment. The front door opens into a lovely sitting room that can be used by everyone on the third floor. Down the corridor to the left you reach Elevator 4. A locked door on the first floor to the left of the elevator leads outside. That's not where Mom parks. She parks in the lot out Door 3. She can see her car in that lot from her windows. The second door in her apartment is close to the back bedroom and bath. Right next to that door is a stairwell only leading down. The third floor is the top floor. There are parking spaces leading from Door 3 and also door 4. Those doors are locked and each tenant has a key. Staff all have pass keys. And who knows how many family members have given keys to their children or relatives. What are you thinking?"

"An escape plan." The idea was being formulated in Rick's detailed mind. "Now how to first find him, get him into Woodfield without being seen, and more important, how to get away from Stoney Lonesome without being followed."

"When should we go to Bloomington?"

"Let's go right now. Whoever may be out there might think we are all asleep. Let's turn out the lights and wait thirty minutes. Then we can slip out without lights on. Get dressed and ready. I'll wait patiently on the porch to see if anyone moves, relocates, or hopefully, leaves. Thirty minutes."

Abby was downstairs and ready to go before Rick came in from his surveillance chores. Abby put an IU sweatshirt over his shirt and he already had Wong's IU skull cap. Abby had on her red slacks, white sweater, and red and white IU vest. They might have to loiter around the gazebo area a long time and they didn't want to look like they didn't belong on campus. A beautiful campus it is, too. Rick coasted down the drive with the lights out and didn't start the engine until he turned right on Rt. 46. It was the dead of night and there were few cars. It was easier to see if anyone was following. No cars were following and few were coming the other way. "What are you thinking about?" asked Abby. Rick hadn't said a word for quite a few miles.

"I'm thinking what we can say if Andy is seen with Alice. With so many people milling about, he might be seen. Alice should have an answer about who he is and why he's with her."

"Couldn't he be her nephew visiting from New York?"

"Yes, he could be that, but then they would expect him to come to the dining room, social hours, etc, with her. It's a very welcoming place and you say they have lots of parties and events. It should be something more secretive, clandestine."

"He is her nephew who is in the Witness Protection Program." Abby was kidding.

"Bingo! Great idea. Then we'd have people helping Alice protect him. Put a little excitement in their lives. Then if need be, he could hide in other people's apartments. Make it a group protection plan. Great idea."

"It is a great idea. I'm glad you thought of it," teased Abby. Her mood was on the rise the closer they got to Bloomington, IU, and hopefully, Andy.

They entered Bloomington on East Third Street, passed by the College Mall, some IU Jacobs School of Music buildings, and on to Indiana Avenue. Abby, navigating, told Rick to turn right, go to the Sample Gates, and then left to park anywhere he could.

"There are gates? What gates? Are they locked?" Rick was unfamiliar with Bloomington, the University, or the University sites and buildings.

"The Sample Gates. They are the official entrance to Indiana University. The face of Indiana University, as it were. The gates are impressive, made of Indiana Limestone, and are the backdrop for many photographs. They are used as the logo for many University pamphlets, invitations, stationery, note cards, and literature. ESPN often films the gates when they are here covering basketball and football home games. So does the Big Ten Network. The gates quickly became the face of IU, certainly the entrance.

Rick did as he was told, turned left on Kirkwood opposite the Sample Gates and parked at the first parking meter on the right. It was too early to feed the meter. Hopefully they would be back with Andy before the meters became hungry. They walked back through the Sample Gates. The limestone gates were impressive with red and white plants blooming in artistic patterns on the manicured ground on either side. The first building on the left was also impressive. That building had originally been the University Library. It now housed the Media School with a sculpture of Ernie Pyle, the World War II Scripps Howard reporter and columnist, at the entrance. Ernie Pyle was an alum and former Editor of the Indiana Daily Student, the student newspaper. Pyle's initials are carved on an old desk he used when he was Editor. The desk is still there. Or was the last time Abby was in the building. Andy and Abby both worked on the student newspaper. They were both in The School of Journalism in Pyle Hall. When Alice was studying Journalism back in the day, the paper was housed in a Quonset Hut. It was close to the Beck Chapel where many students and former students get married. The Quonset Hut was a holdover from World War II.

Abby and Rick kept walking toward the center of campus, called the Old Crescent, and they came to another sculpture. This one was of former Indiana University President, Dr. Herman B (no period) Wells. That no period, she explained to Rick, was strictly for the student newspaper reporters. Dr. Wells did not have a middle name so there need be no period after his middle initial or so the story goes. The story also goes that he was a strong advocate for Freedom of the Press and was always appreciative of the press, particularly his student press.

Dawn was approaching and they were very close to the Gazebo. Both Abby and Rick felt excitement rising in their bodies as they approached slowly, not knowing what, if anything, they might find. They were almost whispering.

"What took you so long?" It was Andy's voice.

He couldn't be seen so Abby pulled up short and looked around. When Andy stood up, she ran into his arms and burst into tears. He held her tight, kissing her head, hair, forehead, and then hard on the lips. He was tearing up, too. Rick stood by quietly observing this unforeseen, unexpected, unbelievable, and unusually touching meeting. Andy pulled away from Abby to look at her, and then shook hands with Rick. "I can't believe you're actually here. My message was delivered and you believed it. I didn't expect to see you, Rick. What all has happened? It's been a long trip. I had to figure out where you might have gone when I didn't find you in LA. I didn't...."

Rick interrupted and said, "Let's get out of here. We may have been followed" They walked side by side back to the automobile. Abby held on to Andy's hand all the while swallowing back tears. And Rick talked idly even though there was no one around to hear. His eyes were darting about, expecting he didn't know what, to appear. They got back to the car and sat for a few minutes explaining what their plan for hiding him was going to be or trying to be. The end result was keeping him safe until the CIA could find and close down Alexandria Bulswiki.

CHAPTER SEVEN

While driving around Bloomington and not seeing anyone following, Rick relaxed a bit and told Andy about his fellow CIA agent friend from LA following some mad scientist, Alexandria Bulswiki. When Rick mentioned his name, Andy tensed up and said, "He's the one who has held me captive all these months."

"Why?" asked Abby.

"He wanted me – us – Ryan and Sam and me, to write and produce a film about him and his efforts to find an antidote or cure for a contagious and deadly virus. He told us that he had already concocted a virus that would infect the world. He considers that a wonderful thing to do. He has come up with some kind of an infectious potion that has the ability to spread infection around the globe. It's his grandiose effort to rule the world. Or somebody's. The more we learned, the more we decided that he was being used by someone else. Evidently this someone else is the one who wants to rule the world and he must be very well connected. Bulswiki is into self-praise and punishes those who don't also praise and obey him."

"His magic potion could wipe him out, too."

"I know, Abby, but he is trying to concoct an antidote that only he controls that would save or cure only the people he wants to save. He obviously thinks of himself as some sort of God."

Abby interrupted, "If he came up with such an antidote, why couldn't other scientists also come up with it?"

"Logic doesn't enter into his thinking. He has one goal and only one goal. He wants to be the one who saves the Universe, and he is planning to do it by bullying and infecting all the people who don't follow his orders, agree with him, and laud him. He is always right. What he says, goes. He's brash, rude, a liar, and often incoherent.

"He sounds psychotic," interrupted Abby.

"He is truly insane. And powerful or whoever is backing him is. I don't know who is behind this diabolical plan. I saw him only once from a distance. He was tall, Asian of some kind, snow white hair and a lot of it, wore slacks and jacket, and had a walking stick. I don't think he needed it. It might have been more for show. He was an imposing figure. I might recognize him if I saw him again. We all three watched him go into the laboratory and pointed his associate to the storage room. Sam got a picture of him, but it was from a distance and the man was turned away from the camera. We never saw them leave. Next morning the helicopter that brought them disappeared. We heard it leave.

"It is easy to manipulate an egotist. Sam, Ryan, and I did it for a long time. It seems someone or some people are using him or are urging him to do their dirty work because he seems to be getting cooperation and clearance for whatever he needs or wants or thinks he needs. And Bull is experimenting on human beings on that island of his using all sorts of dehumanizing tactics and giving them all sorts of tests that either make them deadly ill or deform their bodies and brains to a point that eventually kills them."

"How did you manage to not be one of his guinea pigs?" This was Rick trying to find out what this mad guy was doing and who his associates might be. That must be what Walter and the CIA are trying to find out. It is still a mystery to be solved.

Andy continued, "Bull also has an enormous Ego. He wants and needs praise and glory. He is truly psychopathic. He does the most outrageous things and when they go awry, he blames everyone else. He is praised, mostly by himself, when things go well. And he blames others when they go badly. He is a proverbial liar. He tells one lie after the other and then claims he didn't say whatever it is he said. The problem with extreme psychotics is they actually believe their own lies. And he can't see the truth. He can see a dead person lying there and claim he isn't dead, and I guess he really believes that person isn't dead. The problem is that he appears to be quite normal. He goes out into the real world and associates with people and gets along fine. He seems quite normal and raises no suspicions. I guess people think he is just another odd scientist. They must or else he would be shunned, ignored, investigated and locked up. Then who would think of anyone doing what he is doing. Bull can be charming one minute and viscous the next. He truly is a Jeckle and Hyde. He's a monster."

"Bull?" asked Rick.

"He likes to be called Bull."

"Apologies to Michael Weatherly," Abby added. It was her nature to inject humor into serious situations. This injection went ignored. Or quite possibly Rick and Andy had never heard of "Bull", the one time TV series.

Andy was anxious to get on with his story. He didn't want to be the only one who knew what a horrible person Alexandria Bulswiki was and what horrible things he was doing The information must get out so authorities could put a stop to his activities before he does infect the world. And his friend, Richard Anderson, could certainly alert the CIA.

"How did you get along with him?" asked Abby.

"I played to his Ego. When they hijacked our plane and landed us on some little island, he told us, when we were un-tied, that he brought us here to write and produce a movie for him. I said he'd have to go through my agent. He told us that if we didn't cooperate, we would be given a shot from his secret, deadly cache and we would die a slow and painful death." Andy paused, then added, "Did I forgot to mention that he is also a Bully? A big Bully."

"I believe we got that impression." Rick was driving around Bloomington before depositing his cargo in Woodfield. He wanted to make extra certain nobody was following. "Go on."

"Everyone is afraid of him on the Island. But to continue... then he took us through his hospital, and we saw bed after bed of people dying a slow and painful death. So....Ryan, Sam and I pretended to be writing a movie about his life. Well, we were not pretending. We were really doing it. If we make it through all this, it'll make a hell of a Horror Movie. We were assigned to make him a legend. And we tried. Oh, how we tried. Bull got me a typewriter, a copy machine, and reams of paper."

"A typewriter?" Abby was surprised.

"There is no internet or cell service on the island. There was electricity, but not much else. Not much there. On one occasion, the three of us walked all around the island wondering how or if we could get off. Two of our guards went with us. We had fun that day. Ours was the only commune on the island and it consisted of Bull's not too spacious home, a sparse apartment complex with a dining room where workers in his laboratory and the three of us lived and ate, a big storage shed, the infamous Laboratory, the attached Hospital, and a landing strip. That's it."

"Where did he get his guinea pigs?" Rick wanted to know.

"Every once in awhile a plane would land with people, homeless people we were told, that they picked up on the streets of LA. Probably promised them a place to live, eat, and sleep. Many of them were kept apart from the misfits and evidently not injected with whatever it was that deformed and killed them. After we got to thinking about them and putting two and four together, we decided Bull was going to inject them with the virus and put them back on the streets around The United States to spread the dangerous bug."

"I expect that is how the CIA got on to him. So many street people disappeared. I thought it was following up on your disappearance." Rick was beginning to put the pieces together.

"Where did you three sleep?" Abby wanted to know.

"In the apartment building. We had one big room with three beds, one bathroom, three comfortable chairs, one dresser with three drawers, and a desk we all shared. After awhile he built another building that was our workshop. Our Laboratory, he called it."

"Does he have a family? Wife? Children?"

"He lives alone except for some male servants. And they kept changing. I think if they made a misstep, they would end up as Lab rats. Bull got Ryan amplification material of his choosing and some tools to work with. He got Sam cameras and other photographic equipment. All we had to do is give him a list of the things we needed and somehow, some way, he got everything on our lists. He got us really good equipment. I was supposed to write the script that he checked when he was in residence. He made a lot of changes and added a lot of extra ideas into the mix, all glowing things about himself. After all, he is a genius. He knew he was smarter than anyone else in the world and even if people didn't realize that, our movie would prove that he was truly a legend. He traveled a lot and life was easier when he wasn't around. Even the guards and henchmen were more at ease. I wrote script every day. I made him look like the God he thought he was. He was saving the world from corruption, decadence, and evil. He liked that, of course, and the boys and I kept talking to him about sets, backdrops, actors, scenery, costuming, anything to prolong the process. We told him that movies sometimes take two or three years to make and another long time to get distributed. He wanted names of actors he could approve for the roles and I promised him a list of characters after I finished the script. I said I would make suggestions for casting choices if he so desired. He asked why I was being so cooperative. I told him this was just another job for me. He was the Producer and I was the Director. I wanted the finished product to be as good as it possibly could be. Then he told me to enjoy it because it would be my last job. We knew then that as soon as the movie was finished, so were we. That's why we were being so creative…. and slow. That's also why we began planning our escape."

Andy continued with his story. "With the stuff Bull got him, Ryan pretended he was putting together dual purpose microphones that could be hidden in actor's clothing. Bull wanted to kidnap a costume designer. I told him we needed to wait and see what costumes were needed in each scene. Different designers were better at one type of costuming than others. He had yet to decide where we would shoot the movie. It was a wait and see, cat and mouse, maybe and maybe not existence. Anything to prolong the project. We kept hoping someone would find us, but we were so isolated on the small island and it was so uninteresting and desolate that nobody would make it a tourist stop. We were treated well as long as we pretended we were working. We were working. Ryan was trying to make some kind of electronic device that could broadcast so we could send messages, even code messages, to alert someone that we were being held captive. It was a dangerous move, but Ryan never had the right equipment, so it was never a problem we had to face. Also, nobody passed by to signal anyway. Sam was tinkering with the camera equipment Bulswiki brought him and trying to take pictures of the atrocities that were happening on that island and in that laboratory. Bull only allowed pictures to be taken if he were in them. Such an egomaniac! Sam posed Bulswiki in positions that also showed the atrocities and what they were doing in that Lab and Hospital. Bulswiki was so conceited, he worried about his appearance, not his surroundings," Andy continued. "He was particularly concerned about his molting hair. He glorified the term, comb-over. Only wore tailor-made clothes. He was always in a hurry. He had to rule the world before he was too old to enjoy it, he said."

"I saw him from a distance day before yesterday," Rick said. "He was well-dressed and presented the look of being well-bred."

Andy winced. "You saw him? Here? In Bloomington?"

"In Indianapolis. When Abby called me to come help her find out about the Japanese man killed on her property in Stoney Lonesome…"

"What? A Japanese man was killed on your property? When did you buy that property? I only found out about Stoney Lonesome through a message from a guy I met named Nakazato. Naka worked in a restaurant in North Hollywood. After I escaped from Bulswiki and company, I went to North Hollywood to cash a check at a Bank of America. Thank God you hadn't closed that account yet. I stopped in an I-Hop for something to eat. This Naka waited on me and we got to talking. He told me his sad tale and I enlisted his aid to work on my sad tale."

"What was your sad tale?" asked Rick.

"I told him more or less the truth. I had been kidnapped and I was trying to find my wife and give her a message that I was still alive. I couldn't go because I was on-the-run and hiding from the people who kidnapped me. Thankfully he wasn't curious as to why I was kidnapped. I didn't think he would believe the truth anyway. He was a romantic at heart and trying to find the love of my life appealed to him. So did the money I gave him up front. I'm sorry I put a death sentence on him."

"Why were his fingertips mutilated? Fingerprints were impossible to get. The sheriff tried to find out who he was. He never got your message to me. We only figured it out when Pamfou dug up a piece of paper at the murder scene with my name and Bel Air address on it. He must have found that I had moved to Somewhere, New Mexico, and on to Stoney Lonesome. He must have been quite the tracker." Abby took a breath.

"Then I found a piece of your Hollywood Comedy Club pin and we put two and two together. And then that old lady…"

"And here we are," Abby finished Rick's sentence.

"I was never so glad to see anyone as I was when I saw you two coming up the walk just now."

Abby smiled at Andy and squeezed his hand. She was in the front seat and Andy was sitting low in the back.

"So what's the next move?" he wanted to know. "We can't drive around Bloomington all day. I hardly recognize it. So many new buildings, tall buildings. What are they, apartments?"

"Yes, mostly occupied by students."

"The University must be growing leaps and bounds."

"It is.

CHAPTER EIGHT

Let me tell you what we have planned to keep you safe.

Abby started to explain their plan to hide him. They hadn't actually told him about why they were being so careful. But Andy had found his way from that island to LA to Somewhere to Bloomington. So it wasn't surprising to him that they should be careful. As they learned later, he had used several disguises as he proceeded across the country. He got from Los Angeles to San Francisco to Denver by train. Then as if his luck was holding out, he struck up a conversation with a kid waiting for the train to Indianapolis. Turned out the kid was an IU student and he was going back to Bloomington. Andy offered to rent a car if the student drove. He explained that he didn't have a valid driver's license. He didn't mention that he didn't want to rent the car in his name. The deal was gladly accepted. Andy rented the car in the kid's name and got let out at a gas station on the Southside where he met that old lady. The kid was turning in the car nearby because the rental was in his name.

"Fannie actually got there. I didn't trust her. But she actually got there. Amazing." Andy was beginning to relax a bit.

"Yes, she was last seen having a meal at Abby's. Purity Manor II seems to be the food center for the homeless," Rick laughed.

"Purity Manor II?" questioned Andy.

Abby explained the why of her actions. "Well, you always answered the telephone, 'Purity Manor. Purity speaking'. So I named the house Purity Manor I in Somewhere. And Purity Manor II in Stoney Lonesome."

"Someday you'll have to tell me how you got to Stoney Lonesome. I know how, or why, you got to Somewhere," Andy said. "Now tell me how you have planned to dispose of me safely."

"Please, don't use the word dispose." This was Abby. "Keep. Keep you safe."

Rick told Andy that they had decided to hide him in Alice's apartment in Woodfield.

"The Retirement center the University built?" asked Andy.

"Yes.," said Abby

Rick continued, "Alice lives in a third-floor apartment. It has two entrances and exits for escape possibilities should an escape be needed. There are two bedrooms and two baths so you will have privacy and protection. You are going to be her nephew from New York who is in a Witness Protection program. That's the story her friends and associates will be told. Chances are they will join in keeping you safe." Rick was feeling a little more comfortable, too, since there had been nothing out of the ordinary happening and no one following them. "Ok, we're heading to Woodfield," he announced.

"Just act normal," Rick said as he parked the car.

"I don't know how to do that," said Abby.

"Neither do I." chimed in Andy.

The threesome walked to Door 4, a short walk, and Abby had a key that let them in. The elevator was right there. They got on, went up two floors, got off, walked to an apartment door that had a beautiful floral decoration hanging on it.

"That's Mom's garden," she said as she knocked. She had called ahead reporting their ETA.

"Coming," they heard Alice's lilting voice. "And here I am," she said brightly, opening the door and ushering them inside. She locked the door behind her before hugging Andy. "I hear you are going to be my roommate," she said.

"I couldn't be happier. You are my favorite aunt. And mother-in-law. Always have been." Andy hugged Alice once more.

"As I remember I am your only mother-in-law. I'd better be your favorite."

"Tell me why I am in Witness Protection."

"We haven't figured that out yet. Any ideas?"

Abby thought for a minute and said, "Some case in New York City. You saw the murder and are a material witness."

"The mystery writer at work," said Rick.

"Why New York City?" asked Andy.

"Well, there's always a murder in New York City, isn't there?"

"We can always ask Alexa. She knows everything," kidded Alice.

"Who is Alexa?"

"Oh, Andy, you haven't met Alexa. Show him, Mother."

"Wait. Turn her off. Now. She hears everything and can be our downfall. " Rick was happy someone mentioned that piece of equipment that he felt was like Big Brother. Big Sister, in her case.

"I never thought of that. I don't have her. I think Wong does. We'll make sure he turns his off."

"Is Wong out here with you?"

"And so is Maggie and Pamfou."

"Home sweet home. There were times I thought I'd never see you again."

"I was sure I'd never see you again. I carried your ashes home with me in a very pretty urn. Hey, can you get DNA from ashes?"

"I doubt it. But I wouldn't know." Rick made a mental note to find out from somebody who would know.

"Ask Alexa."

"Mother! Rick, take that contraption away from her." Alice went into her bedroom to unplug Alexa.

Abby, the list maker, sat down at the dining room table and began listing the things Andy would need. An electric razor, toothbrush and toothpaste, under clothes, slacks, sport coat, pj's, and the list went on.

"Who is going to do the shopping?" asked Alice.

"You are," said Rick. "Abby and I can't be seen buying men's clothes."

"Why not? You're a man. Maybe you need clothes. I could be with you and you could be deciding to stay longer and need more clothes and sundries." That was Abby being logical.

"Ok. I guess that makes sense. And you would know Andy's sizes. Actually we are both about the same size. I'm surprised that you look as good as you do, considering what all you've been through. How bad was it?" Rick wanted to know.

"We were well treated as long as we did his bidding. It's what was to come later we worried about." Rick said, as he looked around the apartment. "Where is my room, Auntie Alice? Better yet, the bathroom?"

Alice led the way.

Rick and Abby went on their shopping spree at the Mall. While Abby shopped, Rick kept a close look to see if anyone found them of interest. There was only one other customer in the men's department and he was trying on a tuxedo to wear to a wedding, so it wasn't a difficult job. Rick wrote a check for the final bill, in case someone checked. Then they went to CVS and purchased the other things on the list. Rick added a bottle of Scotch, a bottle of bourbon, and a bottle of vodka to their shopping basket. Also bottles of red, white, and blush wine. When they entered Alice's apartment, they heard laughter coming from the living room. Two of Alice's posse, as she called them, Ione and Maysie, were being charmed and highly entertained by the very handsome nephew, Cary, from New York.

"Cary, huh? I'm glad to finally meet you. I've heard so much about you from Alice and Abby." Good, thought Rick, now we have at least two more people protecting Cary. They hadn't given him a name yet. I suppose Andy was going to be Cary Grant, Rick thought to himself. Andy was enjoying his new role. And why shouldn't he? He was free and no longer weighing each word, each action, and fearing for his life. He had Abby back and he could now see the light at the end of tunnel. Fortunately he couldn't foresee what was along the way to that light.

"Maysie has reserved a table for four for dinner. We can change it to six if you two want to join us. It's Tuesday, wine night."

"Thanks, Alice, but Abby and I need to get back. People are waiting for us. Sounds like fun though."

The girls left to dress for Wine Night. Women liked to dress up for any and all occasions. Men didn't. The best they would do is a shirt, no tie, and maybe a jacket. Clean and pressed is optional. Only time some of them wore suits was if they were going to a funeral. Funerals were not infrequent there and friendships were easily made.

Andy got up to say goodbye and walk them to the door. "Be Vigilant!" Rick warned."

"Thanks, you guys." Andy said as he kissed Abby goodbye. "See you. You don't know how long I've waited to say that."

"Twenty-six months and five days, but who's counting." Abby said, as she and Rick started down to the car. "Life is good again!"

That was being a bit overly optimistic.

CHAPTER NINE

Walter Donnlevy was waiting for them when they arrived back at Purity Manor II. He was in the kitchen with Maggie and Wong eating a piece of Maggie's peach pie with a big scoop of ice cream on it. He was having a hard time because Pamfou had taken a liking to him and kept putting his head in Walt's lap. Walt seemed to like it so Pamfou wasn't called off or locked in another room. The dog jumped up and down greeting the new arrivals.

Neither Maggie nor Wong had told Walter where Abby and Rick had gone or for what reason. He said he was CIA, but they weren't sure if he was a good guy or a bad guy so they were being careful. When the new arrivals walked in Maggie asked, "Mission accomplished?"

"Yes," said Abby, a smile lighted up her face. Both Maggie and Wong smiled broadly at the news.

Walt said, "So....?"

Rick answered, "Yes." He motioned for Walt to follow him. They went outside where they wouldn't be heard, but not before he whispered in Abby's ear, "Don't say anything out loud until we check the place for bugs." She nodded and put her finger to her lips as she turned toward the others. They understood.

"Is he a friend?" asked the cautious Maggie?

"Yes. Well, he's Rick's friend from Los Angeles. Let's wait and see what they have to say when they return. What happened to the lady who came from the gas station?"

"We fed her, and she is asleep in the guest cottage out there." Wong pointed to the west side of the circular drive. "The other bedrooms are occupied. Abbott Hotel is running at capacity."

"I thought she needed to get to Nashville to take care of her sick son. Are you sure she's there?" This was Abby checking up on the details. Abby thought they better keep track of her. She could be easily bribed by Oliver and his partner to tell them what she told us.

"Everything is battened down, isn't it?" asked Wong.

"Yes. Oh, let's wait for Rick and the other guy."

"Walt. He said his name is Walt," Maggie said and then added, "He seems like a nice enough Bloke." Maggie had been in America for many years, but she still used some Irish expressions. She had hardly gotten the words out of her mouth when they heard gunshots.

"Quick, turn out the lights," said Abby and she rushed to her purse and pulled out the can of Mace she carried. It wouldn't deter a bullet, but it might slow down the shooter. More gun shots.

"I wonder if Rick is carrying. Walter may be. We didn't frisk him." This was Wong who watched too many Detective shows.

BJ came running from his room upstairs. "What was that?"

"Gun shots. Someone must be trespassing. Rick is out there."

BJ started toward the door. Abby didn't know what he intended to do and probably he didn't either.

"Don't go out there. Just keep still ..."

Rick stuck his head in the door and told them to lay low. "Abby, hand me my sport coat." She obeyed and Rick pulled a gun from the inside pocket. He already had a gun in his right hand. "Walt thinks he hit one of them. He's going to check it out."

"Be careful," Abby whispered.

"Right." He retreated to the driveway.

The time seemed to drag as they all crouched in the dark room. Pamfou was barking and Wong was trying to quiet him down. Finally they heard a rustling and Walt came in pushing a man and not too gently. After Rick found the light switch, it turned out to be Oliver Gutinov. He had been hit by one of Walt's bullets. Blood was pouring out his right shoulder.

"I'll call the sheriff," Abby said as she reached for the telephone.

"No, wait," warned Walt. "Let's see what he is up to first. We may not want to let go of him. "Do you have a chicken coop or some unpleasant place we can store him for awhile?"

"But I need a doctor," wailed the bleeding Oliver.

"Yeah? What are you going to tell the Sheriff you were doing here?"

"Do you think Alexandria Bulswiki is going to bail you out of jail?"

"Who?"

"Don't play innocent with me," Walt said, "I know you are working for that Mad scientist. The CIA is hunting for him before he infects the whole world." Gutinov didn't blink. Instead he looked puzzled. Perhaps he didn't know what Bulswiki was really up to.

"Oh? You don't know that one of his prisoners escaped and told the CIA what he was really doing on that island of his. When he is through with you, he'll turn you into one of his Lab Rats and shoot you up with his infectious serum. You want me to show you pictures of some of his human guinea pigs? The man is a lunatic. And you are going to protect him? He's sure not going to protect you."

Rick entered the inquisition. "That is what happens to people when their use or value to him is no longer needed. They are dead. We have proof now. Bulswiki is an evil man.

"He…he's a very important man." Oliver became defiant.

"Who told you that? Him? No, that's faux news." Walt released his grip on Ollie's good arm.

"Well, yes, and so did Henry Woodfield. He's CIA and he should know."

"I'm CIA and I do know." Walt was mad now. "Also Henry Woodfield won't be CIA very much longer. He'll be stuck in a cell block somewhere, if he's not executed."

"I'm bleeding to death. Put a tourniquet on my arm."

"Well, we don't want you bleeding all over this nice lady's new home." Walt purposely didn't mention Abby's name.

"New? Whose home is this? Isn't it supposed to be owned by an Abigail Abbott?"

"Actually, it belongs to the Herkleheimer family, from Providence Rhode Island."

"Mr. Bulswiki said it belonged to an Abigail Abbott."

"As usual, Mr. Bulswiki is wrong. It doesn't. This lady only leases it for the Fall Season." Rick said it with such authority, it was quite believable.

Maggie came back with a first aid kit and began trying to stop Oliver's loss of blood. Her Nurse's aide training had come in handy since they moved into Purity Manor II. Her California friends worried that she would be bored to death in a house in the woods in Indiana. Indiana is a state that most of them only flew over. How wrong they were. She had only been here a few weeks and already there had been a murder, a shooting, a trespassing, and CIA agents in the house. Also Abby had turned a very peaceful home into a homeless shelter for Brown County. Or maybe it was Monroe County. Or both. I wonder what tomorrow will bring, she thought to herself. Another boring day at the Ranch? Not a chance.

While Maggie worked on the wound, Walt quizzed Gutinov. "What were you doing nosing around here?"

Silence.

"What information were you supposed to give Bulswiki?"

More silence.

"Okay. Then let's stop treating Ollie here and start dinner. I'm starved, aren't you?"

"So am I," agreed Rick. "Abby and I haven't eaten since early this morning." Before he got that sentence out, lights appeared coming up the driveway.

"That will be Mr. Bulswiki. He was to meet us here. We were hoping to find someone named Andrew Abbott here. You'd better not make Mr. Bulswiki angry. He has a terrible temper."

"Yes, and why does he want Mr. Abbott?"

"I don't know. He didn't say why."

"And you didn't ask?" Rick continued.

"You don't ask questions of Mr. Bulswiki," said the cowardly Gutinov.

Walt left the room and Rick opened the door to see who emerged from the limousine. There was no movement so Rick stepped back and shut the door. As he did so, he also turned off the lights. After a few minutes, Rick told Oliver to go out and see what they want.

"Why me?" his voice breaking.

"Because they are here for you. See what your boss wants."

"I know what he wants. He wants me to bring him this Andrew person."

"Well, tell him there is nobody here by that name. We don't expect him to be here since he is already listed as deceased. And Mrs. Abbott has his ashes on her mantle to prove it.

Oliver Gutinov was then pushed out the door by Rick. He locked the door after the CIA traitor stumbled off the porch. Watching from a living room window, they saw the back door open and a head of white hair appeared in the open door. It was so dark it was difficult to see features for identification. The person was tall, probably taller than Alexandria Bulswiki, but Walt couldn't be sure. Rick had only seen the man once and from a distance so he couldn't be absolutely sure either, but he knew Bulswiki didn't have a head of very white hair. Suddenly Oliver, still holding his bleeding arm, was pulled into the automobile and it sped off.

"There goes our perp," said Walt. "Probably just as well. We know what Bulswiki wants. He wants Andrew Abbott. And he wants him dead."

"I don't know what we could do with Gutinov even if we had him. He hasn't committed a crime here. Well, maybe trespassing. What is your next move, Walt?"

"I don't exactly know. I must get in touch with my home office in LA. Can you keep things running smoothly here? Keep them alive? I will be back in touch with you as soon as I know our next step. I do know we want to capture Bulswiki and put an end to his madness, but we do need to have proof. Andy's word may not be enough in a court of law particularly when we come up against the very smart, very well-connected lawyers that will represent Bulswiki. There is someone very high up, VERY high up, who is engineering this endeavor. Our thoughts on this, and it is only thoughts, not facts, is that whoever it is wants to enter politics or maybe already is in politics. After infecting the country with the Virus, he will come up with a cure and be a hero who is elected to the highest office in the country. Bulswiki himself may be destined for death after his usefulness is no longer of value.

But, as I say, that is what the discussion has been in our office meetings. It has also been discussed, maybe even suspected, that this very important man is connected with Russia. Now the man instigating this is in a holding pattern until Bulswiki comes up with a medication or vaccination or some kind of cure.

"Doesn't sound easy. And it sounds as if we need to keep Andy on ice for a lot longer than we thought. In actuality he really is in Protective Custody." This was Rick adding a post script to Walt's explanation.

"You got it. I'm going back to Indianapolis tonight and try to pick up the trail on the mad scientist and, if not stop him, at least keep track of him."

CHAPTER TEN

As Walter Donnelly was driving back to Indianapolis, his home office texted him that Alexandria Bulswiki had been spotted at LAX heading for Tokyo, Japan. He changed course and headed for Indianapolis International Airport. Walter was on the next plane to Los Angeles. So if Bulswiki was in LA, then he was not in the limousine that picked up Oliver Gutinov in Stoney Lonesome. Even more interesting, who was the white-haired man who roughly pushed Oliver Gutinov into the limousine?

In briefings at the home office in LA, he found out his CIA partner, Robert Thompson, was on that same plane as Bulswiki heading to Tokyo and Donnelly was to join him as soon as possible. Presumably Bulswiki was heading for his Island and they would have to find out just where that Island was located.

Walter Donnlevy met his partner in Tokyo, but Bulswiki had long since departed. Bob watched him board a computer plane for Sapporo. The two men, posing as American businessmen, also went to Sapporo, but there the trail ended. They rented a car at a rental agency and, as luck would have it, while Walter kept the clerk busy, Bob took a picture of the listed rentals for the past week. On it was A. Bulswiki who was to drop his rental in Otaru, a small town north on the coast. Walter rented the car with drop off back in Sapporo. No one could trace them to this place called Otaru in Hokkaido. Fortunately the roads they traveled were good. Following a map they picked up at the Rental Agency, they had no trouble getting there and finding a decent hotel. It was small but clean. Best of all, the hotel desk clerk spoke English or some version of it. Finding food they could eat wasn't as easy, especially when neither man liked or ate fish. But they managed.

At the Rental Agency they were told that Bulswiki did rent an automobile, paid his money in cash, left in a big rush, as if he were late for an appointment.

They followed leads, combined information, and talked to as many people as possible for two days before running into a guy at a private airport in Otaru, a seaside community on the Sea of Japan. Turns out he flies monthly to a small, unnamed island with an odd assortment of things. He described some of the things like test tubes, medicines with names he couldn't pronounce, vials, needles, tubes of all sizes. He used to bring in camera equipment, electronics, and office type stuff, but that stopped a few months ago. "This month there is a lot of fragile stuff," he said. "Can't imagine what they do over there." When Walter asked if they could ride along and check the place out, the man said he welcomed company. He could take three passengers and had taken two people back from there a couple months earlier. "It is really an eerie place," he shuddered. Walter asked if there were many residents on the Island. The man said he didn't see very many. He added something of even more interest than fragile stuff, he said he took a gentleman over there one day last week. It was a one-way trip. He asked the man what was going on over there and he was told that it was none of his business. Not a very cordial person. He was met by several weird-looking people and they took him off in a golf cart. When asked how weird looking, he said one guy had only one ear, his nose was off to one side and he only had one arm that worked. The other arm was deformed. Another guy had no legs at all. He moved on a board that had rollers. Another guy's mouth was badly misshapen and he couldn't talk, only grunt. The pilot, whose name was Dano Martin, decided the island was a place for grotesque people to live out their lives and this man was taking care of them. He had flown this guy back and forth many times during the past three years. Before that there was nobody on the Island and it often flooded and disappeared into the sea. They haven't had many cyclones, squalls, or storms during the past few years.

"We can only hope this doesn't happen until we can get a handle on this dangerous supply of poisonous venom," Walt admitted to his CIA companion, Bob Thompson. "The Seas and Oceans are polluted enough without a poisonous substance being swept into the waters."

"Well, we can't do anything about the weather, and only maybe we can do something about the mad Scientist," Bob said. "I'm more worried about getting off the Island than what we will find there."

"There is that. We should make some sort of plans for what to do when we get there and how we are going to approach the Virus specialist. Or are we going to approach him? Andrew Abbot said this guy is such an egotist and that is how he and his friends kept on the good side of the braggart, also known as the "Death

Provider". And…rescue the third man who, we hope, is still alive and there."

While waiting for the day the next shipment was to leave, the CIA agents outlined Plans A, B, and C. Plan A was for only one of them to leave the plane at first. Bob's cover was acting as a journalist from the Los Angeles Times who was sent there by his Editor to interview the infamous doctor. The CIA office had already arranged that with the paper in case he checked out Bob's cover story. Since Dr Bulswiki already knew Walter was a Fed, it was decided that Robert would be the newspaper man. Could he pull it off? He'd need a lead for his story and that would be that he was told that Dr. Bulswiki was a genius who was about to announce an antidote that would cure a Virus that could kill vast amounts of people. He was going to be the next world-renowned genius who saved the world. Also, they would need a picture or two, perhaps one working in his Laboratory. Bob could take it with the camera app on his cell phone. Or if he had a photographer on the premises, a better picture could be taken. That turned out to be the faulty step in their plan. He should have taken it himself while Sam Walker was being spirited on board the plane with his pictures and whatever equipment he could get on board before someone saw him.

"What if he doesn't fall for that line?" asked Walter. "And what if he suspects you know about the kidnapped photographer?"

"Then come and get me," laughed Bob, but he didn't really think this was a laughing matter. An escape route was vitally important. Necessary, actually.

While Robert interviewed the great man, Walter would hunt for the third man, Sam Walker, the cameraman who was kidnapped with Andy Abbott and Ryan Elliott. Andy and Ryan had both contacted the pilot of the monthly supply plane and were spirited on the plane before it took off. The men decided that Sam was the evil doctor's favorite because Sam took all sorts of pictures of him. Sam agreed but not without reservations. That is how Andy and Ryan escaped, now three months ago. No one was certain Sam was still alive, and Walt's job was to find him and get him back to the plane with pictures. Plan B was to salvage Plan A should something go wrong. Plan C was still an enigma. Both men were in contact with their home office in LA. There was no news.

Everything was quiet on the Indiana front. Proceed with caution was the assignment coming from the LA office. Actually, Langley was calling the shots. If the truth were known, the CIA had been investigating Alexandria Bulswiki for some time now. Word had gotten to them about him developing some kind of poisonous serum over two years ago. Took them awhile to figure out who was developing it. News that Movie Producer and Director Andrew Abbott had been killed in a plane crash caused no red flags to pop up. Not until Richard Anderson notified his Bureau Chief after getting the call from Abigail Abbot, the grieving but suspicious widow. Now the problem had become more dangerous and it had their full attention and action.

Departure day came for Walter and Robert. Fortunately, this was a private airfield in Otaru so no security checks were necessary. Both Walt and Bob had firearms with them and various other protection gear such as Hazmat suits. "Here goes," said Bob, as they lifted into the sky. It didn't seem very far, perhaps a thirty-five-minute flight, before they descended. The place looked barren, and unoccupied. When they rolled to a stop three weird-looking people came out to meet the plane. Dano waved to them as Bob climbed out. They were suddenly wary, but he smiled and said, in English, that he was there to see Dr. Bulswiki. He had an appointment. The newspaper confirmed by phone that Dr. Bulswiki had agreed to the interview. They led him away toward the building that Walt assumed was the infamous Laboratory. Walt and Dano had decided that if Walt was detained, Dano would say Walt was helping unload the heavy stuff. So far nobody else appeared. After a few minutes Walt, carrying a box marked KODAK, walked toward one of the outbuildings. The room contained drum after drum, all standing in a row. Could this be the deadly serum they talk about. Nothing he could do about them now. On to the next building. Sure enough, he found Sam Walker fooling with some camera equipment.

"Sam?" asked Walter.

"Yes?"

"I've come to take you home. Walter Donnlevy, CIA. Andy and Ryan have sent me." He showed Sam his credentials, something he shouldn't be carrying, but he wanted Sam to know he was for real. Just as he put away his wallet, the guy on the roller board came to summon Sam to the Laboratory. He glared at Walt, but Sam told him that this man was delivering a package of camera equipment to him. He offered to show him the Kodak package. Walt, tipped his hat, and proceeded back to the plane to help Dano. Sam went off to the Laboratory with his camera. Things were going according to plan. But were they?

After an hour that seemed like five, Walt saw Bulswiki and Bob walking casually toward the plane. Sam walked slowly behind carrying his camera equipment. Dano also saw the threesome and wondered how they were going to get Sam on the plane with his film without a fight. Suddenly he thought of something.

"I seem to have a problem with a loose bolt in the manifest. Sam, would you have a wrench among your souvenirs? I seem to have misplaced mine," Dano said as he glanced inside to see if Walt was properly hidden from view.

"Sure," said Sam. "I'll get it for you." He started back to his photo lab.

"Wait. Let Dum-Dum get it for you." This was Bulswiki holding Sam back.

"But Dum-Dum won't know where it is and I don't want him messing around possibly exposing negatives and ruining pictures. Our book is about ready for the publisher." Sam started toward his lab.

"Let him go," Bob interrupted. "We need to get away. I don't want to miss my deadline. They have saved half of the front page for my story on you, Dr. Bulswiki, and I don't want it buried on the back pages."

"Ok, but hurry up." Bulswiki motioned Sam to go quickly.

Sam hurried off at a trot. He needed to pick up as many of his film as he could hide on his person. Dum-Dum followed. When they got to the lab Sam began putting film and pictures in a brief case and reels in a sack. He almost forgot to pick up the wrench and he also took a screwdriver. Dano was also in the plane and so was Bob and Walt. Dano started the engine and began rolling slowly down the make-shift runway when Sam, running alongside, threw the briefcase in the plane and made a leap for it. He didn't quite make it and Dano slowed the plane until Bob helped hoist Sam inside. They took off in a hurry. Bulswiki pulled a gun from the pocket of his lab coat and started shooting, but his little handgun couldn't hit the departing plane or so they all thought. They hadn't quite gotten within sight of the mainland before the plane started to sputter. Evidently the gas tank had been hit and they were about to run out of gas.

Dano cut the engine trying to save some gas, but it must be leaking fast. They coasted in as far as they could maintain some altitude before he started the engine again. He was within sight of the airport when the sputtering stopped and they were gliding once again. Thankfully Dano was a good pilot and sat the plane down on a strip of land on the coast. The engine stopped altogether as the plane stopped. The pilot and passengers breathed a sigh of relief as they crawled out of the plane, now tipped over to the right. They began walking toward the airfield a short distance away when they heard gunshots dangerously close by. There were no buildings or trees to hide behind and only two men had guns. They had left the bulk of their protection in the plane because they were carrying Sam's treasured bags of photographs. Sam, the ex-Seal, told them to separate and run in different directions while he went back to the plane for more guns. He zigged and zagged and finally got to the plane without getting hit, possibly because the two CIA men returned shots, hitting one of the two men while Walt, Bob, and Dano ran in different directions causing the shooter to shoot aimlessly missing everyone. The shooter started toward the plane and nearly reached it before Sam found and unpacked a repeater rifle and mowed him down. Sam waited to see if there was a second or third shooter before he rejoined the others. He took other guns with him and handed one to each of his compatriots. How did Bulswiki get word to someone on the mainland so quickly and get a rifleman to greet them. One more unanswered question added to a host of others.

The CIA brought Dano to LA with Walt, Bob, and Sam. They also found him a job flying for FedEx. Dano was retired from the US Air Force and had family in Belen, New Mexico. Hopefully Bulswiki and his handlers would never find him. Actually Dano wasn't his real name, only a nickname. His real name was Daniel T. Martinski II. He said he was lucky they didn't call him Two instead of Dano. Fortunately he maintained his sense of humor.

Walt and Bob took Sam to one of the CIA's safe houses in Los Angeles. After gently breaking the news that Sam was alive and safe in LA, they brought Sam's wife and daughter to see him. Happy and cooperative, his family was content to look forward to the day that Bulswiki and his sponsors were either killed or imprisoned and Sam would be able to safely continue his life with them.

CHAPTER ELEVEN

Meanwhile back in Indiana, Rick was ordered by his Bureau Chief to watch over the Abbotts and keep them safe. This proved to be a complicated job. He couldn't be in both places at once. Either he had to be near Andy in Woodfield or Abby in Stoney Lonesome. He told his Bureau Chief that he needed some backup. If the bad guys couldn't find Andy, they might try to kidnap Abby and try to trade her for Andy. His boss agreed and Rick was sent another semi-retired agent to keep the vigil in Stoney Lonesome.

Abby often drove herself to Bloomington to "visit her mother". To make it believable, Abby and Alice sometimes went out to lunch in downtown Bloomington.

Alice liked the Malibu Grille and Abby liked the Uptown Restaurant. Other times they went to Simon Mall to shop and eat at Applebee's. They tried to make it look as normal and as casual as possible. Abby parked and entered Door 4 and left by the same door.

Sometimes she stayed over.

Rick Anderson had let it be known to Alice's friends that Cary, her nephew from New York, was indeed being held in Protective Custody. Rick was the Federal agent who was protecting Cary and who was also courting Alice's daughter, the widow Abby Allison Abbott. Now with the reappearance of Andy Abbott, that was the closest Rick was going to get with his love for Abby. Andy and his mother-in-law, aka Cary and his aunt Alice, invited Maysie, Ione, and Joyce to Alice's apartment for wine and cheese. Rick explained to the ladies what was going on and what might happen should Cary's whereabouts become known. He tried to impress them how well connected and dangerous the murderer was back in New York, the one going on trial for several murders, one which Cary witnessed.

"It just happened that Cary was at the right place at the wrong time." Rick explained. "The people sent to eliminate him, a witness, were professional killers who might stop at nothing to attain their goal, even shooting innocent bystanders. So...be vigilant and be careful."

All the ladies agreed and were fired up about the prospect of excitement and perhaps danger. Now they had an assignment and were gung-ho to accomplish it. At times Rick wished he had not included them in the protection detail. Often they were too gung-ho. He had learned from Alice who her friends were and about their background.

Maysie and her twin sister, Daisy, were born in El Paso, Texas. After college at Southern Methodist University, Maysie went to New York City to job hunt. Her hunting paid off. She started as a File Clerk at a NY Advertising Agency and retired thirty years later as a Vice President in charge of Casting for commercials, both print and video. She had been retired for over ten years and had lost her husband seven years ago to a massive heart attack. Then she closed out their retirement home in Sarasota, Florida, and moved to Woodfield to be near her daughter. Her daughter was a Professor in the Media School at Indiana University in Bloomington, IN. She taught Investigating Reporting.

Rick's ears perked up hearing that. He warned Maysie that she should not tell her daughter about this because it may be too interesting for her to keep quiet and not get a big scoop. A scoop might result in getting the murderer free and the witness dead. Although Maysie disagreed and was certain her daughter would keep the news to herself, she agreed not to tell her about this assignment for the safety of all concerned.

Maysie was persuaded it would be a better story when they had an end result.

Ione had a different background and upbringing. She was a farmer's daughter and grew up on farms in Missouri and Kansas. She married her High School Sweetheart and raised two children, a doctor and a scientist, and resided 50 years in a home they built in a suburb of Kansas City. She was a homemaker, fundraiser, and community leader. After the death of her husband she moved to Woodfield to be near her daughter, a Pediatrician in Bloomington.

Rick wasn't worried about Ione.

And then there was Joyce. Joyce had married a performer who, because of necessity, became a performer herself. She had been educated at Indiana University and with a degree in Journalism, entered the field of Public Relations in Chicago. Her first job was as Assistant to the Advertising and Publicity Director at the world's largest hotel at the time, The Conrad Hilton. Six months later she became the Director and worked closely with

Conrad Hilton himself. Six years and two National Democratic Conventions and one National Republican Convention later, she married one of the performers in the hotel's Boulevard Room floor show. She formed a production company with her husband, traveled the world booking, publicizing, and performing in the very popular Family Fun Shows. Upon the sudden death of her husband, she returned to Bloomington to live near the Aunt who raised her. When the Aunt died, Joyce moved into Woodfield. Joyce said she proved the old saying, You can't go back home, untrue. She maintained moving to Woodfield was one of her wiser decisions.

The three ladies and Alice melded right away. Mostly because they each have a wild sense of humor, are basically optimistic, and find so many things to enjoy together.

As Alice liked to say, "Birds of a Feather flock together."

So that was Rick's "Security Team". Alice, Ione, and Maysie all lived on the third floor. Joyce lived one flight down, across from the back stairwell next to the back door of Alice's apartment. Rick gave each of them his private number in case there was an emergency and he was needed but otherwise occupied.

He spent most every day with Andy playing cards and discussing the details of the case or just visiting or hiking around the Woodfield campus. On some of their hikes they were joined by Maysie on her roller skates and Ione with her walking sticks.

Both Andy and Rick were amazed that a seventy something lady still roller skated. They were told that Maysie had a twin sister, Daisy, back in Texas, and they had given each other roller skates on their seventieth birthday. Unfortunately Daisy had fallen and sustained a broken wrist, but that had not deterred

Maysie. Daisy's husband, older but still of some common sense, confiscated Daisy's skates and gave them to a neighbor's child.

Maysie kept hers and oiled the rollers periodically.

On those walks the foursome laughed and kidded with each other. It was an outing Andy looked forward to. Rick enjoyed the strolls, too, but was not as at ease because he was cognizant about his whereabouts. Both men had handguns should there be a surprise intruder pop up. With Maysie along there was always a funny story or some comical event that gave them something to tell the others about on their return to Apartment 329.

Andy and his mother-in-law, aka Cary and his aunt, began going to dinner in the beautiful dining room. Tuesday was wine night, and on Friday there was a Social Hour before dinner. They pretty much ate with Alice's friends. Rick didn't think it wise for Abby to be seen with Andy. The wrong people might get the right idea that this unknown person was Andy Abbott. So instead of his wife, Cary enjoyed dining in the company of Alice, Maysie, Ione, and Joyce. People began calling them Cary's Harem. The women, of course, were quite pleased and enjoyed the company of the charming gentleman who was in the Witness Protection Program. Ione, who lived across the lounge from Alice, was especially watchful for any strangers who might wander by. She always had a knitting basket beside her while she sat inside her open door, although keeping apartment doors open was frowned upon. She was knitting a sweater for Cary while eyeballing the lounge and hallway. Since theirs was the last wing built onto Woodfield, not many strangers visited the third floor and there were only nine apartments up there. Once when Ione didn't recognize one of the maintenance staff, she confronted him and shooed him away. After checking with the Maintenance Director and finding out this stranger was a new employee of the Maintenance Department, Ione allowed him to go to an apartment down the hall to fix some leaky plumbing.

"So let them think I am a psychotic old woman," she explained to the others while defending her actions.

Suddenly the lounge outside Alice's front door became quite popular with the ladies. They changed their bi-monthly Book Club meetings from the Card Room on the lower level to the third floor lounge. They had a jigsaw puzzle set up permanently on a card table that became a fixture. Rick couldn't be sure, but he suspected the ladies took turns working on the puzzle so at least one of them was there much of the time. As predicted, casseroles showed up on the little end table beside Alice's door. To Rick's surprise, although as an afterthought he wondered why this should surprise him, objects like a baseball bat, an ugly vase, an iron skillet, and a basketball showed up around the lounge area and within reach of the couch, card table, and comfy chair. He even found an old rusty handgun stuffed between the pillow seats of the davenport. The gun was so dirty and stiff from rust that it would never fire, might even backfire. Rick retrieved it, cleaned it, loaded it, and put it back where he found it. Just in case. Either whoever put it there never checked to see if it was still there or forgot where she put it. Rick noticed there was a lot of forgetting going on.

On Mondays, Wednesdays and Fridays Andy and Rick went with Alice to Exercise class at ten o'clock. Andy was assigned to a position by a back door that led outside. They both kept a close eye on the others, but there were no strangers joining the class. While Alice went to Yoga and Balance classes Andy stayed in the apartment with Rick. They were working on writing down all the things that happened on the Island. It was sort of a diary of events as well as Bulswiki's activities and conversations with Andy, Sam, and Ryan. In short, they were building a case against the mad scientist should he be brought to trial.

Andy actually enjoyed living in Woodfield Retirement Campus with his mother-in-law and the many visits with his wife. As he always did, he was trying to make the best of the situation. When Abby stayed overnight on Mondays and sometimes on Thursdays, Andy and Alice and Abby and Rick dined together as a foursome. The three lady protectors ate nearby at a table for four. They all, minus Abby, sat together at the Friday night Social Hours. Rick kept an eye out for anyone who may have crashed the party. It would be easy to do. Anyone could come in the front door, get in the hors d'oeuvre line in the Fireplace room, pour themselves a glass of wine or take a can of beer from the ice container and join a table in the Founder's room or the Terrace room. So far nothing suspicious had happened at the Friday night gatherings. It would have been more questionable if Andy didn't attend.

Word, of course, had spread through the campus that Alice Allison had a male relative living with her. As gossip gets twisted, reasons for his appearance here ranged from hiding from a Chicago mafia thug or an irate husband to being a witness to a murder. The last bit of information overheard in the mail room was closer to the truth. People liked this mysterious nephew and accepted him into their midst no matter what or who he might be hiding from.

So far so good. Rick's concern was they might all get complacent and let down their guard. But the ladies kept their vigil. That was proven a few days later.

On a Tuesday night two couples had dinner together in the Woodfield dining room. Alice and Cary and Abby and Rick. Alice reported there were quite a few guests dining. Well, of course, it was Wine Night in the Dining Room. Each resident earned up to four freebies a month when and if they missed dining themselves. On Tuesdays and Fridays they had to pay for guests. The same with special dinners/parties like Oktoberfest, Chinese New Year's, Oscar Night, Indy 500, Mardi gras, and any other special nights dreamed up by the Activities Director. There were many.

On this particular Tuesday night Alice recognized some family members of her friends and pointed them out to Rick. Others she couldn't explain, but according to Rick, none looked suspicious. Anyway, it was nice relaxing and enjoying a good meal and a glass of wine together. Rick, his back to the wall with a good view of the entrance, was joining in the conversation, laughed in the right places, and was attentive to Abby. They were supposed to be a couple, as far as Alice's friends knew. Abby noticed Rick eyeing everyone being seated by the Hostess, the lady who joked and kidded with them. Abby wondered if Rick ever really relaxed. She decided that it goes with the territory when you are in a dangerous profession. She made a mental note to use that in the next script she wrote. She smiled to herself. She assumed now that Andy was alive and well, they would continue in their own professions after this was over. The others saw her smile and asked what she was smiling about.

"Just enjoying the atmosphere, the company, and the wine." Little did she know that all hell was going to break out very soon.

The foursome walked up the back stairs to Apartment 329. Rick led the way and as he opened the door to the third floor he heard voices yelling, one a male voice. He quickly opened the back door to Alice's apartment and ushered in Andy and the two ladies. He pulled a gun from the back of his trousers and proceeded up to the lounge area. He saw a man down on the ground with little round plump Maysie bouncing on his chest. Ione had his coat pinned to the carpet with her knitting needles, and Joyce was threatening him with the iron skillet. Now we know who armed the lounge with threatening utensils. Rick rushed to their aid, pulled Maysie off the intruder, and pulled the intruder up, all the while holding a gun on him. Maysie handed Rick a gun, saying she found it stuck in the back of this man's pants. That was before Joyce hit him with the iron skillet. Rick pushed the bleeding, bleary-eyed man down on the couch and shooed the women away. Forgetting that he put the gun between pillows in the couch, Rick returned from closing Alice's front door to face the gun in his face. The man pulled the trigger but Rick dodged aside and shot the man in the chest. The other residents on the floor came rushing up to see what the commotion was about. Showing his CIA credentials, he said this dead man was sent to kill Cary, who was in Protective Custody. They believed him because they had heard all sorts of rumors about who the nephew was and why he was at Woodfield. Besides, they knew and liked Cary. They even felt sorry for him for having to go through all this and especially for having to fear for his life for doing the right thing.

So the attempt on Andy's life had been averted. Still....how did they know Andy was here? Or maybe they didn't. Maybe it was just a reconnaissance assignment. Well there wouldn't be any information reported from a dead man. Rick had his CIA coworker take care of the laundering. He immediately dialed Purity Manor

II in Stoney Lonesome. Help came and the problem was solved. Nothing untoward had happened in Purity Manor II. Yet.

Three days later Abby returned to Woodfield. She had awakened with an eerie feeling. She couldn't explain exactly how she felt. It was a nervous churning in her stomach. After being up and around for awhile, she shook this uncertainty off. Abby bid a goodbye to everyone and left on her twenty-seven mile journey. She hadn't gotten much further past the entrance to Brown County State Park when a van came very close to sideswiping her. She veered out of the way and honked her horn. The van slowed down, then sped up, and then came to an abrupt stop. She managed to slam on her brakes before rear ending the stopped vehicle. Seeing a man with a gun jump out of the back door, she sped around the van and barely made it into her own lane before slamming into an oncoming car. She raced toward Bloomington hoping to get the attention of a State Policeman. Unfortunately no police car was spotted along the road watching for speeders. Racing through red lights attracted no police. She drove down Third Street and turned into the Police Station. When she did that the Van continued on. Instead of reporting this incident, she continued on to Woodfield using side streets. Nobody followed her.

This news scared both Rick and Andy. It was decided that Abby would not return to Stoney Lonesome. She would stay in Woodfield. Now both Abbotts were in Protective Custody. They would figure out an explanation to the residents and staff later. Rick thought the Bulswiki group was trying to kidnap Abby and trade her for Andy. It had been mentioned during CIA conversations as a possibility.

It so happened that about that time Kat drove over to Stoney Lonesome because she could not get in touch with Abby. Wong or Maggie always had some excuse for Abby not being there. Rick thought it was best that Kat not know about Andy's return or whatever else was going on for her own protection. If Abby's phones were tapped and they found so many calls from Kat, the bad guys might put two and two together and visit her for information. Once there, it was decided that Kat should stay there and pretend to be Abby while Abby was in protective custody herself in Woodfield. If people were watching, they would see a woman , a man, and the house guests all going about their business as usual. Nothing different, nothing suspected. Even though the house was tested for bugs, all the information was exchanged on walks among the trees. Kat had been brought up to date and got daily reports from Bloomington. She readily agreed to the plan. Not a person who spooked easily, Kat was glad to have the other CIA agent living with them.

CHAPTER TWELVE

There had been no news from Walt. No word that they had gotten Sam off the island or even had gotten themselves back safely. No news is good news, they say, but that didn't keep Rick and Andy from worrying. Rick kept in close touch with his home office, but they had no word either. The last report was that the two Feds had found a plane and a pilot to fly them over, and a departure date had been set.

Andy also wanted to find out where Ryan was located. Or relocated. Word came that the CIA had him sequestered away from his family. Knowing Ryan as he did, Andy was sure Ryan would find a way to see his wife and their two growing children, hopefully not putting all of them in danger. Ryan kept saying he was sure his kids wouldn't recognize him. He had grown a full beard and a moustache and lost twenty-five pounds.

Bulswiki was so determined to find and kill the escapees and had such good contacts in the United States, safety was very uncertain. Andy, putting two and two together, was certain the contacts were highly placed and extremely dangerous. Professional killers were possibly tracking them all down right now. Rick surmised that since the safety of the entire country was at stake, several Federal Agencies would be called in to find either Bulswiki or his handler. Or both. None of them would be safe until that happened.

Andy worried about Sam, his Director of Filming; Rick worried about Walt and Bob, his co-workers. Andy kept saying that Sam was very smart and would keep his cool with the Bull. He was a big fellow, a retired Navy Seal, and quite capable of taking care of himself. Rick knew that two CIA agents were assigned to get Sam off the Island. They all hoped that would happen, but no one knew just what kind of furor would be raised if Sam went missing.

"Bull has a vicious temper and is prone to do all sorts of wild things when aroused. I only hope Sam takes some of his pictures with him."

"That was uppermost on Walt's mind." Rick promised to keep Andy apprised of news on the outcome of that venture. But no news had arrived.

"What language did the inmates speak?" asked Abby, four weeks into Andy's seclusion at Woodfield.

"Mostly Japanese. In our spare time Rob and I were teaching English to the inmates who were involved with us. Bull spoke English to us and Japanese to the others. And the LA Homeless hostages spoke English or Spanish, of course."

"Bull spoke enough Japanese to make himself understood. Quite a lot of Japanese actually. He cursed them out in English.

Once I overheard him talking on his ham radio to someone in Russian."

"Was he mean to them?" asked Abby.

"Aside from causing them physical and mental harm with his experiments, he wasn't mean to them. Unless he was having one of his angry tantrums. Then he threw whatever he was close to. Books. Dishes. Glassware. We were not allowed in his Laboratory, but once in awhile we heard glass breaking. Then we knew he was having problems with his experiments."

"How many people did he have working with him?"

"Only himself and three assistants. All chemists. He, the Genius, didn't want to share any glory that he predicted would come when he saved the world. Presumably the associates would be eliminated when the project was completed."

"Oh, God. I hope the CIA guys haven't been detained." Andy fretted.

"Andy, if they have been, CIA will send in an army to get them out. Let's stop wondering and worrying. There is nothing we can do about it from here."

Something else the contingent in Indiana didn't know was that the CIA was formulating a plan to land on the Island and take Alexandria Bulswiki into custody. It took them over a month to agree on a plan, gather the troops, and round up the equipment and resources. CIA had to check with Washington, DC for permission to include the Feds, the Marines, and the Navy Seals. Sam, safely back in the USA along with Walt and Bob, had been called back to the Seal Team that was assigned to swim ashore. He was familiar with the Bulswiki compound and could lead the hunt for the mad scientist. Finally it seemed they had all their plans in order and D-day was scheduled for October 19th.

A ship would take the Seals to a mile away from the Island, drop them and wait for their return. A plane loaded with Marines equipped for battle would parachute onto the Island on the other side of the Bulswiki compound. Timing was of the utmost importance. They did a mock invasion on another island far away from the actual invasion. All went well with that one.

What they didn't know was that somehow word got back to the wrong people about the planned invasion and when the Marines landed on the island, they were met by a well-armed armada of resistance. It was truly a battle between the opposing forces and would have ended badly if the Seals hadn't risen from the sea and increased the odds on the winning side. The Seals were supposed to find and capture Bulswiki but were delayed fighting the opposition. During that time somehow, from somewhere, a helicopter appeared and whisked Bulswiki away. So the offensive was successful in that all the barrels of the infectious serum were confiscated, but Bulswiki got away to where, no one knows.

Suddenly a no-named island in the middle of nowhere became a beehive of activity. Bulswiki's three assistants were captured and returned to Washington, DC, where they were incarcerated. It was hoped that they could provide the formula for the poison and work with American Scientists to provide an antidote or vaccine for the infectious liquid. Only one of the Chemists refused to cooperate. He remained in jail. The other two were more than happy to offer their knowledge and help. They were invited to work with a team of Scientists at Eli Lily Company in Indianapolis. They wore tracking devices and were locked down in an apartment near the lab where they worked. Bulswiki and his handlers would certainly want to do away with both of them. And maybe even the third one in jail. A team of FBI Agents were stationed in the building with them in Indianapolis for protection. The hope was they could capture the intruders sent to do away with the scientists. It was in the hands of the FBI coming on board in the United States.

One of the FBI agents got word from an informant that the building was going to be blown up one Saturday night, killing everyone inside. That was averted when one of the agents found and defused the bomb a short five minutes before it was to explode. And the search went on. Bulswiki, the hunter, now became the hunted. The CIA wanted to capture Bulswiki and confiscate the poisonous product before it became a deadly pandemic that spread around the world. Miraculously, all this had been kept out of the press. The product was secured but not the man – or men – responsible for it.

What the Federal Agents were trying to do was find out who was bankrolling and responsible for this heinous crime and stop any further action by this person. After becoming aware of some of the scientist's shortcomings, they decided to play to his ego. Their plan was formulated and one of the agents dressed as Bulswiki made the rounds of the Talk Shows and News Shows as well as interviews to the print reporters. A Hollywood makeup artist did a great job and the fake scientist went on camera declaring that he had failed at trying to come up with a pill that would slow down the aging process. He was quite humble and open about his failures and lack of scientific knowledge hoping that the ego-driven maniac would come out of the woodwork to deny ever saying such things and be captured. Whatever was going on undercover by the agencies was not known by the group protecting Andy. Three agencies were involved and actually cooperating. Each group had their assignments and were proceeding accordingly.

A DOD agent found Bulswiki safe – though obviously not sound - in Russia. A NCIS team was dispatched to capture and get him back to the United States. That was underway, though not completed.

The Indiana contingent was busy keeping the Abbotts alive. The kidnapping attempt of Abigail Abbott was not successful. That did not mean there would not be other efforts to get her as a bargaining chip to trade for Andrew Abbott.

Time drew long and it was beginning to wear on the participants. Waiting for news that was slow to come caused more and more frustration and fear. Abby was now permanently living in Woodfield. Her friend, Kat, was evidently permanently living in Purity Manor II. This was to show the enemies that Abigail Abbott was still living there and without her motion picture Director husband. Or if they didn't believe that scenario, then the Abbotts had leased out their newly constructed house that also included the staff to another couple. Whatever they believed, the car that was often parked at the foot of the long driveway stopped showing up.

Life at Stoney Lonesome continued without any problems. Dr. Bob found Fannie a job cooking at one of the restaurants and she had moved in with her son, the son nobody believed existed but was glad that did.

The patient, Hilda Hanson, recovered and stayed in the big house. It was decided the more the merrier - and the safer - if there were more people around. Bobby Joe, or BJ as he liked to be called, entered school in the Fall semester. After taking some tests, he was put in the eighth grade. He was an eager student: eager to learn, eager to make friends, and eager to make good grades. He used Abby's address and was given all the proper shots by their now daily visits from the handsome Dr. Robert Austin. Dr. Bob could no longer make plausible excuses for coming to see Hildy as her doctor. She had recovered and was thriving on Maggie's cooking and care. He was now coming as a Beau because there was no doubt that he was infatuated with the very pretty Hilda Hanson. He sometimes took Hildy out on a date night. Maggie, like a Mother Hen, stayed up waiting for their return home from an outing. No intruders were seen since the limousine picked up Oliver Gutinov, now seven weeks ago. The CIA agent Rick requested to protect Purity Manor II while he was at Woodfield, was now living in the Guest Suite not occupied by Rick Anderson. His name was Jason Riffey and he was actually retired from the CIA but "On Call" when needed. He was a widower, tired of retirement, and welcomed any emergency call he got from the agency. Of the old school of detectives, he was quite thorough, very suspicious, alert, and all business.

He was standoffish at first, until Kat Hastings made it her goal to get Jason laughing. Determined to pull Agent Riffey out of his doldrums, she started kidding him. Then they talked. Well Kat talked. Jason listened. At first he didn't know how to take Kat and her constant jocularity and good mood. It wasn't long before he joined her in inane conversations and even added some nonsensical retorts of his own. Soon they laughed at each other and later laughed together. They became friends.

John Wayne Wong had started work on a Ph.D at Indiana University and was doing research and taking classes at SPEA. His presence in Bloomington also kept him in close touch with the Abbotts in Woodfield. Both Abby and Andy Abbott were very proud of their adopted prodigy. He was the liaison between both factions in Indiana, even though there was little news coming their way.

Woodfield kept its residents occupied, busy, entertained, and fed. It wasn't long before the group in Apartment 329 was accepted and considered in the fold. Evenings in Stoney Lonesome were spent watching movies on the big TV in the Den. Kat chose mostly comedies and, from the outside, it appeared that this was just a happy family enjoying their time together. While appearing not to have a care in the world, they were nonetheless always on guard for intruders. It was all waiting and wondering what would happen next.

CHAPTER THIRTEEN

Another thing they didn't know in Indiana was that a NCIS team of four had entered Russia on student visas in search of Bulswiki but had not yet located him. Deep under cover as university students, they had only one name that might be able to help them. Boris Lenderoff. They were trying to find this person. They dare not ask about him. They didn't want to put him in danger, and they certainly didn't want to blow his cover. Or theirs. Evidently Boris had been entrenched in Moscow for a long time.

The only clue they had is that he often frequented a certain neighborhood bar near the University. So the foursome, usually separated in pairs, also spent a lot of their spare time hanging around this bar. To keep up with their excuse for being in Russia, they had to go to classes and turn in assignments.

Two of the NCIS agents were given Russian names: Ron Romanoff and Sylvia Checkov. The other two were Kevin

Smallwood and Barry Hallsworth. Their Los Angeles office had taken care of all their credentials and background information should anyone check. Of course they were thoroughly checked. They were even interviewed separately before they entered the school. Fortunately, they knew each other's fake backgrounds because they were supposed to be friends. They evidently passed with flying colors. Their colors were red, white, and blue.

The American agents had two pictures of this undercover CIA guy, Boris Lenderoff.

His name could have changed but not likely his appearance, although Plastic Surgery, like many other surgeries, had improved quite a bit over the years.

"Patience, my friends," the American Fed faux-named Kevin kept suggesting to his Coworkers. Co-hunters, as it were. So much time, so little accomplished. They were getting antsy.

One evening there was a brawl in the bar and the police rounded up all the customers and took them into the station for questioning. The four agents were not involved in the melee nor had they witnessed the fight so they were released, but not before they recognized one of the policeman doing the questioning. It was Boris Lenderoff. They dare not speak to him there, but Kevin and Barry waited around until Boris got off his shift and followed him home. Boris was not contacted at his home because they noticed that someone else was also following him. Watching from a distance, they watched this unknown person try to grab Boris from behind. Boris was ready for him. In one swift movement he landed a punch on the assailant's throat, stabbed him, and walked him off into the shadows. They themselves remained out of sight and watched an automobile pull away from the curb and speed away into the darkness of the night. It was then that Kevin and Barry approached Boris. At first they acted like two drunken students singing an American popular song, popular at ballgames anyway, "Sweet Caroline". Holding each other up, they sauntered beside Boris. Barry pushed Kevin into Boris knocking him inside the open door. "We are NCIS from the US. We need to talk to you." Barry made sure Boris wasn't going to strike out at them, too.

Unscrewing the light in the already dim hallway, Boris led them up one flight of stairs to his apartment. Inside the men shook hands, and Boris asked, "What are you doing here?"

"We are here trying to find an individual wanted back in the States," said Kevin evasively.

"Alexandria Bulswiki?" Boris surprised them with the name.

"Are you looking for him, too?" asked Barry.

"No, but I was told to expect a couple of Agents from NCIS that were looking for him."

"Actually there are four of us, but we are getting nowhere. We are here as Exchange Students at the University. We can't ask questions of anyone, and we were told you were the only person we could trust to help us."

"Kevin, is it? Kevin, I don't know how much help I can give you. His whereabouts seems to be top secret. My informants say they hear he is here in Moscow under serious protection, but they can't find out where. I would say the University is a good place to start, but it is still a needle in a haystack. What kind of help do you need?"

"Weapons, for a start," answered Kevin. "And any information you have – or get – would be helpful."

"Where are you staying?"

"In a Dormitory with the other Foreign Exchange students." Barry put forth that information. "We are never alone. We have to check in and check out. They are watching our every move. There are people watching who we talk with, who we eat with, and where we go and with whom. We are allowed to go to that bar you raided tonight, but there are people keeping tabs on us there, as well."

Kevin continued for Barry. "We have to go to class and turn in assignments or else we would be sent back home. One of our team is a lawyer and he does our assignments for us so he is busy in our dorm room while we can slip out once in awhile."

"I will get an apartment for you near me here. Maybe even in this building. How will I get information to you? We can't use cells, texts, or email. They even check up on the local Politsiya. I am under surveillance myself."

"Yes, we know. You were followed tonight? He was ahead of us and we saw the little interaction you had with him. We also watched two men in a car that sped away after you killed him."

"That was no man, Barry. She was a woman, a very skilled member of the KGB.

They think I saw them poison one of Putin's dissidents. Actually, I didn't, but getting proof of such poisonings is my current assignment so I was there. Or nearby."

"You aren't safe, even as a politsiya?" remarked Kevin.

"I haven't been safe for going on eight years here. I can't let down my guard for a minute. The CIA only contacts me when there is an important assignment. This Bulswiki project is evidently considered important."

"It amounts to worldwide Germ Warfare. Yeah, it's important. Hundreds of thousands of people will die if it isn't stopped in its tracks." Kevin was dead serious.

Boris continued. "The Russian hacking problem is being assigned to a couple other CIA implants. They are much younger and computer geeks. One is studying at the University. I'll try to contact him. Maybe he can get in touch with you. His name is Igor."

With all that said, the threesome bid each other goodbye with promises of getting in touch somehow at the bar. Getting an apartment outside the University made no sense and they would have no excuse to live off campus so Kevin declined that offer.

Three days later, with still no results or contacts, a young man crawled on a barstool next to Kevin and Barry at the popular bar. At first his conversation was quite innocuous. "Exchange students?"

"Yes," said Kevin. "You?"

"No. I have temporarily moved to Russia. But I was born in the States, educated there, and moved to Moscow after college."

"Why?" asked Barry, who joined in the conversation.

"To further my education. I majored in Russian at Duke University. Thought it would be interesting to study further in this country," explained the young man who introduced himself as Igor. "I am also at the University. Surprised our paths haven't crossed."

All the while the three students talked, Igor doodled on his napkin. Igor left abruptly, pushing his half-empty glass of beer and the napkin toward Kevin. Thanking Igor, Kevin poured what was left of Igor's beer into his own and took the napkin. While he didn't look at it right away, he made sure the napkin got into his jacket pocket before they left the bar. Kevin and Barry gathered up Ron and Sylvia and started walking the short distance to their dorm room. Around the corner from the bar they were picked up by a Politsiya car. It was Boris Lenderoff. He was introduced to Ron Romanoff and Sylvia Checkov. Boris had checked out his police car for any surveillance material, found and removed a following device and a microphone recorder before picking up the foursome. He not only had firearms and ammo for them, he had information that Alexandria Bulswiki was sequestered in a suite at the Marriott Moscow Grand Hotel located at 26/1 Tverskaya St. Boris drove them by the hotel as he talked so they could get the lay of the land. The hotel was big and built right on city streets. He drove them around the back to where a loading dock was located. He finally dropped them near their dorm.

Kevin told Boris they could not take the guns and ammo with them because they were searched as they entered their building. Boris asked if they remembered where he lived and both Kevin and Barry said they did. He gave Kevin a key and said the weapons would be in his apartment when they needed them. He explained they would be hidden in an open space behind a removable wall panel underneath a Klee original painting in the dining room. They would be in a black carrying case with a false bottom. Barry got out of the police car first and noticed an automobile lurking half a block behind with lights out. He began staggering and weaving into the street as Boris drove off. Quickly his partners followed his actions and blocked the way so Boris could get away. After one of the men in the car tailing them pulled a gun and got the drunken students back on the sidewalk, they sped off. They hoped Boris saw the activity in his rear-view mirror and got "lost".

Now they had some planning to do. But where to start?

The Americans were quite careful talking in their dorm rooms and their classrooms. They also carefully checked for mikes and cameras hidden in their clothing each time they dressed. The only time they felt safe discussing plans was when they were outside eating breakfast or lunch. The four usually ate alone sitting on benches at one of the metal tables. They made a practice of doing this so it became natural and unsuspecting. They ate at different tables each day so no pattern of behavior could be detected. Two days after the Bulswiki information came to light, Igor walked by. Kevin yelled at him. "Hey, Igor. Remember me? We met at the Bar the other night."

Igor stopped, paused as if trying to remember Kevin, then said, "Oh, yeah. I do remember. Good to see you again." He walked over to shake hands with Kevin and Barry and was then introduced to Ron and Sylvia. When asked to join them he reluctantly sat down.

Jovial conversation followed between the five students before Igor delivered the message he came to deliver. "The CIA has arranged with the University for Kevin and Barry to get jobs at the Marriott Grand Hotel. They were both told to report for work on Saturday, two days away. Kevin would be a bellman and

Barry would work in the kitchen. Now that he had met Ron and Sylvia and would ask his source to try and get Sylvia a job in housekeeping. Ron would remain at school doing all their assignments.

"Shouldn't we get told about the jobs by the University?" asked Kevin. "How can we just show up? Who told us to come? We don't want to get you involved with us."

"By the way, we can't read the message on the napkin. What sort of code is it? We've tried everything we know? Unfortunately, we are not analysts."

Over his shoulder he whispered, "Monopoly." And he was off.

Ron excused himself and said he had work to do in his room. The others made themselves visible in case some University official wanted to talk to them. Sure enough, it wasn't long before they were all summoned to the Registrar's office.

They were told, not asked, to report to the Marriott Grand Hotel for work. "We don't need to work. Our college costs are being footed by scholarships," Ron complained.

It was explained that the Marriott Grand was frequented by English speaking people and the hotel asked the University to supply English speaking students to work there part time. The Registrar pointed out it was a courtesy extended by the University, and students would get full credit for doing so, as well as postponement of final exams.

And so the four, not just three, went to work at the hotel the next morning. Plans were being formed and proximity to the target was getting closer all the time. Kevin worried about how they would capture Bulswiki with all the security around him.

Even if they managed that, getting him out of the hotel and the country and back to the United States for prosecution would take flawless timing, and very good luck. Definitely not an easy task. But they were NCIS and they would find a way.

As luck would have it, - or was it luck? - Sylvia, in housekeeping, was assigned to Bulswiki's floor. Kevin was a bellman stationed in the lobby. Bellmen stood in a line in front of the Registration Desk and took turns helping guests with whatever chore they wanted done, not just toting luggage to rooms. Barry was assigned to the kitchen. Since he was low man on the totem pole, he was relegated to delivering Room Service. That got him around the hotel. He, too, got familiar with the halls, doors, and shortcut routes. Ron was assigned to the Chauffeur desk that included parking, driving, and going on errands. His station was a small enclosure off the front entrance. At least they were spread out in the hotel.

Kevin asked the head bellman if he could have a tour of the hotel so he could know where he needed to go. He got a thorough tour by the Director of Public Relations up to and including short cuts, locked and unlocked doors, and back and side entrances. This proved to be a very advantageous tour by a young woman named Martina, who thought Kevin was a Hunk. Kevin did nothing to discourage her.

Even in her maid's uniform, that she had altered to fit tightly over her already sexy body, Sylvia was a beautiful woman. This was noticed by the Bulswiki Protection team. They struck up a friendship with her, kidded and laughed with her. She was always welcomed by Bulswiki's security. She never saw Bulswiki. One time a man came to the door and asked one of the men for the morning New York Times newspaper. Sylvia offered to get it for them and they allowed her to do that. Upon her return the guard was away from the door so she knocked. A very tall, distinguished man with snow white hair answered the door and took the paper from her, but not before she took a picture of him with her cigarette lighter. Sylvia smiled sweetly and said, "You're welcome," even though he hadn't thanked her. This man didn't look like a Security person. Instead he was elegantly dressed, and appeared to be a CEO of some big company or perhaps a Motion Picture Company Executive.

Sometime later Kevin saw the tall, white-haired man Sylvia mentioned check out of the hotel. Kevin took a picture of him, a better one than Sylvia got with her lighter. Also his name on the register list was: Charles Ko from Taipei. Probably an alias. He probably had many fake passports in different names.

Ron had finally decoded Igor's message on the napkin. It was the names of two businessmen who were registered in the hotel: Steven Colston and Donald Schultz. So far they hadn't been spotted. But Kevin kept trying to get a peek at the hotel guest list and finally found out that Steven Colston was registered in Suite 411. He was listed as Vice President of PepsiCo. Kevin made a mental note to deliver something to his room. He had Boris send a package to the hotel. Kevin intercepted it and delivered it to Mr. Colston. Unfortunately, the suite was empty, but Kevin asked around and found that Mr. Colston had a private plane that was parked at a certain section of Vnukovo International Airport. Good to know. While the four exchange students landed at Vnukovo Aero port, they were met by a university official and driven back to the Campus. Kevin had no idea in what direction the airport was from the University, much less from the Marriott Grand Hotel. Boris would have to be their GPS.

A plan could not be completed before a lot of loose ends were tied up. Sylvia was instructed to locate one of the big laundry containers and know how to get it when needed. Ron was supposed to locate a laundry truck and figure out how to steal it from the fleet of trucks from the company that serviced the hotel. Barry was supposed to somehow get knockout medicine into Bulswiki's food or drink. Kevin was the messenger between the NCIS people and Boris and Igor. Igor procured a syringe and the drug Propofol from a student friend who worked for an Ophthalmologist. It was a drug used in eye surgery to produce rapid onset of sleep with a rapid awakening. It had exactly the effect they wanted to have on Alexandria Bulswiki. Unfortunately, it had to be administered through injection and not in the food or drink. No date had been set yet, but the plan was beginning to form.

Barry, Ron, and Sylvia went about their duties at the hotel as usual. Sylvia found a big canvas laundry container on wheels. It had no cover but she had filled it partially with dirty laundry that could cover an unconscious body. She hid it in a closet in one of the housekeeping locker areas on Bulswiki's floor, locked the door and kept the key.

Ron had the opportunity to drive around and chart an escape route. Also he staked out a Laundry truck from a fleet of trucks from the laundry company used by the hotel. If it was seen at the loading dock, no one would suspect that it didn't belong there. Being the experienced Federal agent that he was, he prepared for a backup in case plans went awry. As a precaution, he staked out a smaller truck with no lettering on it. He hot-wired it, filled it with gasoline and parked it in a parking area not far from the hotel. He also left the gloves he was wearing to avoid fingerprints. Every now and then he checked to see if the truck was still there.

Kevin had been in contact with the PepsiCo Executive, Steve Colston, who turned out to be undercover for the DOD. Donald Schultz had been called back to Washington so it was just Colston there to initiate plans. The plane had been sent there for that very reason: to whisk away Bulswiki along with the federal agents. So…. all the loose ends were finally tied up. All Systems GO!

The date was set, but circumstances provided an earlier departure. One of Bulswiki's Security inside the Suite asked Sylvia if she would watch the Scientist while he and his associate grabbed a bite to eat. She said she would in a couple of minutes. She had to deliver some dirty laundry to the loading dock and she had to get the laundry cart first. The others were alerted. Ron got the truck. He got the unmarked truck he stashed in case of emergency because it was the closest to the hotel.

Barry picked up a tray of food and said he had to deliver it to the Bulswiki Suite. Before he was allowed down the corridor one of the security men checked the food on the tray remarking how good it smelled and how hungry he was. Barry said the menu in the Employees Cafeteria was especially good today. The hypodermic needle filled with Propofol was in his pocket, hypodermic needle stuck in a cork from a wine bottle, and a gun was stashed in the back of his pants.

Kevin alerted Boris right away and also Steve Colston. Then he delivered two pieces of luggage that contained some serious gun power. The bag was marked "Bulswiki Suite. Private." Only he didn't take it to the Suite. Instead, he delivered it to Sylvia and they hid the contents in the laundry cart she had sequestered in the closet she locked.

Sylvia was the first to arrive to relieve two of her Security friends. There were two others stationed at each end of the corridor. She waved at them and entered the room pushing the laundry cart that also contained the guns. She smiled sweetly at Mr. Bulswiki sitting at his desk. He barely acknowledged her.

When Barry sat the tray of food down on Mr. Bulswiki's side table, Barry deftly uncorked the needle, stuck it into a vein in Bulswiki's wrist, and pumped its contents into the surprised scientist's arm. It was all done so fast Bulswiki didn't know what happened. He soon keeled over. Barry caught him before he fell and he and Sylvia, who had emptied the cart of the guns, ammunition, and dirty laundry, dumped him into it. They covered him with laundry and made certain he nor the heavier fire power could be seen under the dirty linen.

Kevin knocked on the door and stepped in to leave a package just inside. Before he withdrew from the open suite door, he noticed Barry and Sylvia strapping a gun in holsters on their legs. He knew the more powerful weapons were hidden underneath the dirty laundry with the Scientist. When he stepped back out he said, "Have a good afternoon." Using his key card, he locked the door behind him, in case someone got curious. Then he headed down to the loading dock.

As they pushed the cart out into the hall, Barry called back, "You're welcome. Enjoy your lunch." He and Sylvia parted at the end of the hall beside two relaxing Security men. Sylvia pushed the laundry cart. Each found their way to the Loading Dock.

Boris, in his police car, was already there when Ron backed the truck up to the dock. It was only a few minutes, but it seemed like an hour, before Kevin, Sylvia, and Barry showed up. They rolled the laundry container into the truck and Barry and Sylvia stayed inside with Bulswiki. Kevin climbed in the front with Ron. They took off with a police escort.

The ride to the airport was uneventful. Boris knew exactly how to get to the Private Plane section of the airport. Steven Colston had the plane warmed up and taxied out to the end of the runway. Hopefully he had taken care of making the flight plan and getting ready for takeoff. Boris led them directly to the plane. Ron positioned them so the back of the truck could not be seen from the row of buildings on the far side.

Since there was no window between the truck and the cab, Barry and Sylvia couldn't see how close they were to their destination. Kevin evidently realized this and when the plane was in sight, he knocked on the truck, a signal to Barry. On cue, Barry helped Bulswiki out of the cart. He was still groggy and wobbly. Sylvia on one side and Barry on the other, they walked Bulswiki to the steps of the plane. The NCIA agents and their police escort, Boris Lenderoff, then climbed on the plane that had started to move a bit before the stairs were pulled up and locked in place. And they were off.

There was a chorus of cheers from the passengers.

"That was easier than I thought," Ron said.

"We're not out of the woods yet," Kevin warned. The mood got quieter, and the hum of the plane's motors lulled some of them to nod away. Bulswiki began to wake up and come alive.

Before he could ask questions, Kevin explained that his friend, Mr. Ko, had sent them and his private plane to bring him to a safer place than the Marriott Moscow Hotel. That seemed to appease him and he drifted off to sleep again.

— ◦◦◦ —

Colston had charted the plane to St. Petersburg, a city where he had flown many times, supposedly on business. They would refuel there and return to Moscow, only from St. Petersburg they would fly on across the Gulf of Finland to Helsinki. Hopefully, no suspicions would be raised. If someone wanted to board the plane to check on things, he would say that his co-pilot had a very contagious disease and they would be returning to Moscow immediately. Always thinking ahead.

It happened that someone, actually two people, demanded to come on board and pushed their way aboard. They were immediately overwhelmed by Kevin and Ron and thrown back on to the tarmac. The steps were hoisted and locked in place and Steve Colston took off into the wild blue heading southwest. When they were over the Gulf waters, there was a general sigh of relief. They had hardly exhaled when they were flanked by two Russian planes. How could they have reacted so swiftly? Where was the leak? It had to be Alexandria Bulswiki.

Sylvia searched his pockets and clothing. There was a tracking button on his shirt. It was crushed and Bulswiki was brought to the front and belted into the co-pilot's seat. He could be seen by the fighter pilot on the right and hopefully they would not be shot down. Colston signaled that he would follow his captors who veered away, only Colston's plane continued forward. They were out of Russia now and shooting down an American plane over Finland would create a national incident. No shots were fired and their plane landed safely in Helsinki.

Now what?

# CHAPTER FOURTEEN

En route across the Gulf of Finland, Steve Colston asked the Helsinki tower to have someone from the American Embassy on hand when they landed. He wanted that person to come on board before any of his passengers deplaned. He was told to taxi to a certain gate which he did. He was also told that no one from the Embassy had arrived yet.

"Is he en route?" asked Colston.

"We are told that he is en route," came the reply.

"Then we will wait on the plane until his arrival."

"But Sir, you and your passengers would be more comfortable waiting in our lounge. We have food and beverage and comfortable seats."

"We are quite comfortable on the plane, thank you. In the meantime it would be good if you would refuel our plane." Colston wanted to get in and get out of Helsinki before anyone knew they were there. Possibly they already guessed Helsinki was their destination out of St. Petersburg, but could they get an assassin team there that fast. Possibly they could. And maybe they did.

A different voice said, "Sir, we cannot fuel the plane with passengers still on board. You must know that."

"Oh, sorry. I wasn't thinking. We are in such a hurry to get on to our destination that I jumped the gun." Steven Colston answered.

"Gun? Gun? You have guns?" the original voice sounded alarmed.

"No. No guns. That's just an old American saying that means I jumped before I thought."

"You jumped? Sir, there are no stairs. You are at the gate. No one is jumping."

Colston shrugged his shoulders in resignation. "No. Of course not. No one is jumping. How close is the Ambassador?"

"I'll check," came the answer. "But I wish you would deplane while waiting."

Kevin wouldn't rule out anything in the discussion of where it would be safer: on the plane or off the plane. While that decision was being discussed, a knock came on the exit door. Four NCIS special agents jumped up, guns pointed at the door.

"Who is it?" asked Colston.

"It's your Uncle Sam. Let me in," the voice whispered. Louder he shouted, "I'm the mechanic. We noticed something leaking from the tail of your plane. I need to see what it is. You may be grounded until I check it out."

"Are you alone?" asked Barry.

"Quite alone," came the response.

Kevin nodded and Barry unlatched the door. The mechanic entered. Barry motioned him in and noticed there were several people standing there. He put his gun out of sight of the onlookers. Barry also noticed the onlookers were all in suits, some carrying clipboards. It appeared they were airport officials. But then that could be a cover. Nothing could be ruled out. This case was far from over.

Once in the door that was closed and relocked, the mechanic looked around and said, "Not very many of you. Hey, is that you, Jake?" He pointed to Boris.

"George Lohrman. What are you doing in Helsinki?" Boris clasped George on the back, as men do. To the others he said, "Lohrman is CIA. We worked some cases together back in the day."

"I'm here for the same thing you are evidently. Getting some scientist back home again to the good old US of A. That Taiwanese Industrialist has people all over the globe. I saw three of them eating at Subway inside the terminal just now.

"Subway? They have a Subway here? What I wouldn't give for a Sub about now." Ron was the one who was always hungry.

Ignoring Ron's interruption, Kevin asked, "What did you say? A Taiwanese Industrialist? Is he the one pulling the strings on this?" Kevin was all ears. "Is he tall, well-dressed with a crop of white hair? Is his name Ko?"

"I don't know. I have never seen him. I only just heard about him. His name was never mentioned to my knowledge. One of our agents captured a couple of guys trying to poison the drinking system of one of our CIA safe houses here in Helsinki. They told the interrogator that their boss was a very important factory owner in Taipei and that this man would get them out of jail. Only he didn't. I was told that both those underlings were squealing like rats until the office where they were being questioned was blown up and everyone inside that room was killed. Whatever information that hadn't been transmitted was lost. That's all I know."

"So we know Bulswiki's backer has people already entrenched here and you saw two of them here in the airport?" Barry was factoring that information into his escape plans and not on the plus side.

"Yes. The CIA has been tracking them for awhile now. But now to the problem at hand. Do you have a plan for getting out of here alive?"

"Not exactly. Do you?" Barry relaxed his grip on the gun still in his hand.

"Not exactly. But I have been working with the Ambassador, rather the interim Charge d'Affaire. He has agreed, if you need it, to give you asylum in the Embassy until our government can get you all out safely along with the mad scientist.

"That's all well and good," said Barry, "but how are we going to get to the Embassy?

George continued. "They say the Embassy guy is en route, but I heard there was an accident on the bridge blocking all traffic. My suspicions are that the accident was no accident, only a delaying tactic. I hope I am wrong."

"If that's the case, maybe the sooner we move, the better. Before they can get their troops here." This was Kevin, although he didn't sound convincing.

"I don't like it, Kev," said Barry. "Still….I don't see any other alternative. We have to deplane before they give us fuel and we can't go on without refueling. Or at least we can't get very far. "

"Colston, how far can we get?" asked Kevin.

"I'm looking at the map. I don't really know where other landing fields are, at least with fueling capabilities for big planes like ours," was the answer.

"What about a smaller plane already fueled?" asked Ron.

"But how far can a fueled up small plane get us," Kevin wondered.

After a moment of silence, George Lohrman said, "Let's get off the plane here and take our chances of getting to the American Embassy. We can be air lifted out of there in the dark of night. I've already lined up two vans, hopefully one with a few armed friends, and maybe we can get away before the assassins arrive in force. Colston, you taxi out to the far runway ready to take off. I'll get the big vans out there. Actually I have armed vans on the tarmac already, just in case. And I have two others for decoy close by. You can make the transfers out of viewing range from the airport buildings. They won't know which van the scientist is on. Of course they could blow up all the vans. You're call."

"So what are we going to do?" Sylvia asked. This was the first time Sylvia, the female undercover NCIS special agent, entered the conversation.

Sylvia was probably the most dangerous sniper shooter this team had. She was also smart, strong, tough, and beautiful. Usually she was partnered up with Ron, who acted like a smart ass while always behaving like the smart, wily federal agent that he was. He insisted his inane talking was to calm down situations and lessen tensions. Most times that worked for him. Right now, even he wasn't feeling very talkative.

Kevin was the leader of the team while Barry was the strong-arm whose ingenuity was keenest of them all. They all loved, respected, and trusted each other, although you would never know it by the way they jibbed at each other all the time. Theirs was maybe not the most straight-as-an-arrow team, but they were the most successful. They had gotten people out of foreign countries before. The Powers-that-be hoped they could pull this caper off, too. It was of utmost importance to national security. Ostensibly they were on their own. Supposedly the government knew nothing of their intrusion into a foreign country.

But to answer Sylvia's question, the undercover mechanic answered, "I will leave and say I need a whole new piece of equipment in order to fix the problem. I don't think my cover has been blown, and I'll supposedly go out to get this equipment. Instead I will get the vans moving in the direction of the plane and try to be on one of them. You start to taxi as soon as you can. If I am asked what is happening, and I probably will be, I'll say, "I don't know, but they won't have a bathroom on board. I hope no one took a laxative." There was nervous laughter.

"What should I tell the tower?" Steve Colston was already heading toward the cockpit.

"Tell them you have just been called back to St. Petersburg." Kevin answered him.

What if they don't believe me?"

"Does it matter?"

"Gotcha. What about my co-pilot?"

Kevin told Sylvia to get Bulswiki ready for the transfer. Barry can carry him if necessary. But get him in one of the vans with Barry, me and Boris. Ron, Sylvia and Steve will go on the other van. Hopefully there will be armed agents in both vans."

"The more the merrier," said Ron, as Kevin unlatched the door letting the mechanic out. He also told the entourage that the pilot was told to taxi out to the far runway and that is where the installation of the new commode would take place. He told them that so the stocks would be removed from the wheels.

Steve Colston started the engine, revved it up, and proceeded to taxi toward the end of the farthest runway. It was also nearest to a gate leading out to the highway. He pulled at the brakes to avoid a collision with a plane landing in front of him. Good thing Steve was an experienced Navy Air Force pilot. He made sure the exit door of his plane was on the side away from the airport.

Steve taxied slowly avoiding other plane traffic at the extremely busy airport and ignored the excited voices from the tower who were switching incoming planes to other runways and turning planes back. He didn't understand any Finish language but he imagined that some of the words that were directed at him were not of real help in his departure and would probably make the sensitive blush.

George's plan was put into action. The time seemed longer than it was but no vans were seen moving toward the runway. That may have been part of the plan. Vans would be driven into position after the plane was in position to hide them from eyes in the terminal. Seems George thought of everything. Or did he?

Barry stood ready to open the door and deploy the chute for the escape from the plane. He wanted verification that the vans were en route before they deplaned. Sylvia, with Bulswiki in tow, reported seeing several vans coming toward them. Kevin slid down the chute first followed by Ron and Boris, then Barry took over with Bulswiki, and finally Sylvia and the pilot. Side doors of the van were opened by armed men and the group jumped in, separating as they had discussed. Barry and Kevin were with Bulswiki. Ron, Boris, Sylvia and Steve were in a second van. George Lorhman was driving the one with Bulswiki and the two NCIS special agents. As they sped toward the airport exit onto a thoroughfare two more vans joined in between, leaving the Bulswiki van second in the row.

They had driven about a mile and a half when a big truck sideswiped the first van. George veered out of the way, as did the other two. They heard gunfire as they proceeded toward the American Embassy. Kevin, riding up front with George, noticed a black sedan with dark windows following and passing the other two vans until it was close behind the Bulswiki van .He alerted Barry who opened the back door and shot the front of the sedan. Smoke came out of the hood and it spun out of control crashing head on into an automobile coming the opposite way. While it was a hair-raising drive no other attempts to divert the entourage were made. The gate of the Embassy was open as they approached the compound. It was a cold, formidable structure encircled with what looked like limestone walls with spiked rods atop.

Kevin noticed the Finland police were on hand. He wondered if they could be trusted and he hoped the United States Government had briefed both the Charge d' Affaire and the Finish government about the situation. Steve Colston had been in contact with his DOD officials all along the way. Hopefully the Rescue Party wasn't out in the cold. Yet.

Two vans proceeded through the gate that was closed and locked behind them. The other vans proceeded on down the street. It was followed by one of the Finnish Police cars. Behind those protective walls the passengers got out and were ushered inside.

Both Kevin and Steve explained their situation and asked to call their home bases: NCIS for Kevin, DOD for Steve and CIA for George. Caught up on their whereabouts and positions, the home bases said they would get back to them at the American Embassy in Helsinki. They were told to cool it until arrangements for their removal from the country could be arranged. Above all else, keep the Scientist safe.

They were assigned rooms, two people in each. The NCIS foursome took turns staying with Alex Bulswiki. They were on first name basis with the captive by that time. He had taken a shine to Sylvia. She had spent the most time with him and had begun to ask about his youth. She had tried other subjects of conversation, but talking about when he was a little boy growing up in Poland seemed to calm him the most. Sometimes she even had him laughing. They seemed to be on a friendly basis. They had received word that complimenting him and massaging his ego was the fastest way to gain his confidence. Sylvia was the best at doing that.

Kevin and Barry spent time explaining to him how they were sent to protect him. They wound a story around the tall, white haired man named Mr. Ko from Taipei who had sent an assassin team to kill him. Their Agency got wind of the plot and the four of them were sent to Russia to make sure he was not killed. So far, so good they said.

When Bulswiki asked why, he was told that the United States wanted to hire him to make a vaccine to thwart a certain germ that had been found on some Island in the Sea of Japan.

"How did they get that?" Bulswiki wanted to know.

"I haven't the faintest idea," reported Barry. "I would imagine the CIA had an undercover agent there. Everybody got all unstrung and our agency was brought in. We were told that a Scientist named Alexandria Bulswiki was noted for his vaccine serums and the United States wanted to hire him and his staff to come to Atlanta, Georgia, to find a vaccine for this particular germ before it was unleashed on the world. You will be a hero if you do, known around the world actually."

"Really?" Bulswiki brightened. "Then why can't we just go to Atlanta?"

"Because this person named Ko has put out a contract on you. For some reason he wants you dead. That's why the government has sent us to make sure you get back to the United States alive and safely."

"I thank you for that. Was I not safe in Moscow?"

"No. That is where that Ko guy was staying. It was presumed that he had a team of assassins at his disposal," Barry explained.

"But I was being protected there." Bulswiki couldn't get it through his head that his so-called sponsor was the villain who wanted him dead.

"Yes, you were. By Ko's people. I'm surprised they hadn't killed you before we got into the country and found you." Kevin took up the explanation. Barry was exhausted trying to get through the thick skull of the Scientist. Was it thick or wary?

"It took awhile for us to get clearance to enter the Country." Kevin continued.

"What country?" Obviously Alexandria Bulswiki still wasn't thinking on all cylinders. That was not unusual after his several infusions of that anesthesia.

"Russia. They are very strict about letting Americans in." Bulswiki answered Barry's question. "How did you get in?" Suddenly his mentality appeared sharper.

"They brought us in as employees of the hotel. The hotel didn't even guess that we were there under false pretenses." Barry wasn't going to give up the way they really got into the country. He didn't want to risk putting suspicion on the hotel in case the hotel was needed for favors in the future, in case Bulswiki told that story to the wrong person.

Kevin and Barry weren't sure Bulswiki bought into that tale. I guess that question will be answered in the future. For now they were just waiting anxiously and suspiciously for their next set of instructions. Waiting. And waiting.

CHAPTER FIFTEEN

The protection contingent in Indiana was also taking it one day at a time and was completely unaware of what was going on in Russia and now Finland. Evidently it was on a need-to-know basis. Since the intrusion on the third floor, there were no other sightings from strangers or other suspicious occurrences. Life was going on in Woodfield as usual. After her attempted kidnapping, Abigail had moved into the apartment with her mother, husband, and their CIA protector, Rick Anderson. Abby and Andy were already working on a script for a motion picture about a mad scientist. Why not? There was not much else to do.

Then one Friday night during the Woodfield Social Hour, a fire suddenly broke out in the garbage room on the third floor. Two of the third-floor tenants were late going down to enjoy the wine and snacks supplied by the Activities department. They decided it would be faster taking the back stairs rather than waiting for the slow elevator. They saw smoke coming out of the Garbage Room, investigated and called for help. Maintenance and Security put out the flames that hadn't spread to the walls, only the plastic tubs that held papers, cardboard, and boxes. The flames were put out before the Fire Department arrived to ensure no live embers remained.

The siren was heard in the Party Room and Rick left to check on it. His heart sank when he saw the fire trucks parked at Door 4, the only elevator to the third floor. By the time he got there to talk to a fireman, the situation had been resolved. It was determined that a lady two apartments down from Alice had been smoking cigarettes although she had been warned several times that there was no smoking anywhere on the Woodfield campus. She swore she was not smoking, but no one believed her because she had defied the rules so many times before and all the neighbors knew it. They could smell the cigarette smoke coming from her apartment and on her person. When her children came to visit the smell changed to the smell of Pot. The lady got the blame this time, but Rick wasn't convinced. Of course, he suspected everything, attributing it to a possible attempt on Andy's life or Abby's kidnapping. He said nothing and everything calmed down on the third floor. He was alert the rest of the evening and slept aware of every little creak and groan of the old building.

A couple days later Rick heard from Walter Donlevy that a NCIS team had captured Bulswiki in Russia and had spirited him out of Moscow but was stranded in Finland. So far they were being protected in the American Embassy in Helsinki. Seems the CIA and even England's MI6 were trying to get them safely out of Finland. At the last report no plan had yet been formulated. The news was slow in coming and progress seemed to be even slower. Walt promised to keep in touch when he could.

It was a waiting game.

It was a waiting game in Finland, too. Sylvia spent most of her time with Bulswiki. Kevin and Barry were in conference with their director. Steve and Boris were in touch with their people. And the Embassy people were in touch with their federal bosses, too.

George went back to work at the airport after checking to see if his cover had been blown. Evidently it had not or the CIA would not have condoned such a decision. They needed an agent embedded at the airport and so far George had raised no suspicions. Back at work he showed up with a new toilet and fixtures, surprised that the empty plane had been confiscated. George wondered if and when someone would realize there was nothing wrong with the plane's toilet. In case someone did discover that, he should have a story ready. He would plead guilty of taking a bribe from someone to keep the plane from leaving Helsinki. Perhaps the worst that could happen is that he got fired. The enemy is the one who wanted to keep the plane from leaving, so maybe the whole thing will be forgotten or, at best, dropped. Still, George was cautious.

It was decided that they needed eyes on the outside of the Embassy grounds. So Ron was spirited out of the compound in the Laundry truck that made daily deliveries. Actually the laundry truck driver was a CIA operative so Ron could come and go without an excuse. The driver provided Ron with a dog and he walked the dog up and around the bordering streets. He noticed automobiles, license plates, and people. No one paid attention to a guy dressed like an ordinary Finn walking and playing with his dog.

The dog Ron called Finny was friendly and snoopy. He approached people and made many stops to sniff and smell. The stops gave Ron time to look around to see if anybody was sitting in cars, particularly parked cars across and down from the Embassy gates. For three days in a row, one car was there with the same two men inside. Ron wondered how they always got the same parking space. Did the car stay there and the men come in shifts? Ron walked by at about the same time each day so it wasn't unusual that the two men were the same. On the next day Ron went by early, about sunrise. This time he walked on their side of the street and stopped to acknowledge them. It was a different man and a woman this time. He spoke to them in Russian. They automatically returned the greeting in Russian. Ron and Finny proceeded on their way, but Ron was certain they were surveillance on the Embassy and said so to the team.

Kevin was worrying that the longer it took for them to get out of Finland, the more prepared the enemy would be to stop them. It could be a blood bath and nobody would come out the winner. He kept in touch with his NCIS Director warning him of the obvious. His orders: Stay put. Stay safe. Don't move until instructions come. Still no plan had been passed along to them or so it seemed.

SECNAV, the White House, and several agencies were furiously planning a Finland escape and a return of Alexandria Bulswiki to the United States. A massive man hunt for the Taiwanese Industrialist, Charles Ko, was underway. With his connections, he could be hiding anywhere. No doubt he had been forewarned about the interest in his whereabouts. He would have a lot of help hiding and being sequestered out of sight.

The Media had gotten wind that Ko was a person of interest, even if they didn't know exactly why. His picture was on the news and in newspapers everywhere. Of course, social media had all sorts of information crowding the Internet, none of it correct but stated as factual. People believe what they read or hear. This might or might not be helpful in locating the tall, white-haired Industry mogul. At any rate, the search was on-going.

What started out to be a United States case has now turned into an International one.

CHAPTER SIXTEEN

Word finally reached the compound in Finland that plans for their escape were being formulated and the date of their departure would be on October 31st. Halloween in America.

"Are we all going to be in costume and masked? wondered Ron.

"No matter what costume he wears, Bull will be noticed because of his height. He's even taller than Barry," persisted Sylvia. She was now on a first name basis with Bulswiki.

"He's so thin, he can be a skeleton." This was Boris assigning costumes. "I want to be a Ghost. Sylvia, you can be an Owl. Ron, you have to be a Witch on a broom."

"I thought witches were all women. I never heard of a male witch. Sylvia is a Witch. I'll be a wise old Owl." That was Ron adding in his two cents.

"You are not that good an actor to portray a wise-old anything. And I am not a Witch." Sylvia thought for a minute. "Only once in awhile. When a gun is pointed at me."

"Calm down, people. This is serious business. Whatever they tell us to do, it will be dangerous, and timing will be of the essence. So calm down." Kevin was serious although he knew they were just blowing off steam after sitting idly waiting for instructions for days.

Instructions finally came. They were brought to the Embassy by George Lohrman, the airport Maintenance man, aka CIA, who got them out of the airport and into the Embassy. Gathered around Lohrman with pad and pencils in hand, they were all anxious to find out their next move. Following was the plan George laid out:

1. Around 4 pm on October 31st, a bus load of children all dressed in costumes and masks, carrying sacks they hoped would soon be filled with candy, would be admitted inside the Embassy grounds.

2. When the festivities were over, the children would return to the bus and sit by the windows laughing and squealing like they came in. The seven adults would be squeezed onto the bus, sitting on the floor in the aisle between the seats.

3. The bus, driven by George Lohrman, would come out after a few minutes and proceed to the northwest. They would drive around until it was certain no one was following. Then they would head to the Vantaa Highway Strip where a Finland Military plane would be gassed up and waiting for them.

4. In case they were being followed, the Finnish Police would apprehend and take the people following into custody. They would be held until word came that the American party had departed the country.

5. At the airport the adult passengers on the bus would be off-loaded and loaded onto the military plane and flown to London.

That was the end of Finland's preparations and instructions. Now it was time to begin putting those instructions into action. The American special agents began donning their assigned costumes. Lohrman waited by the gate until the bus load of kids arrived. Instead of one bus there were two. They parked beside each other waiting for the gates to open. That wasn't the plan. He did not open the gates. He hurried back inside to confer with the others. People inside the Embassy kept a close eye on the buses. Nothing happened for a few minutes, then the doors opened, and gunmen jumped out shooting at nothing but the empty courtyard.

Kevin said, "Maybe they will run out of ammo. Let's just wait them out."

One of the braver shooters tried to climb the wall but didn't make it. Another tried and did make it to his chagrin. The electric wires on top of the wall executed him. He fell backward into the street. It wasn't long until they retreated into their buses and left.

Now it was time for different plans to be made. Agents and the Finish police got their heads together and were knocking around different ideas when another bus appeared. Was it another bus or one of the same buses? It was the bus they were expecting because it was loaded with excited children. Lohrman went out to open the gates.

Quickly the agents got back in costume and Sylvia put a bullet proof vest under Bull's skeleton costume. It seemed he believed Sylvia and the others, especially Barry whom he seemed to like, when they told him they were there to protect him because Mr. Ko had put out a contract on him. Kevin wondered if Bull was really convinced. Perhaps he was slyly letting them think he believed them. Still iffy, as far as Kevin was concerned.

Lohrman stacked guns and ammo in the bus while the others played with the children. There were games, balloon fights, lemonade, and ice cream enjoyed by all until the Spaceman (Kevin) announced that it was time to leave. Ron ushered the kids back on the bus and the other costumed adults came on behind them. Sylvia sat behind the skeleton in the middle of the aisle. The friendly Owl was in the back with Barry and Kevin in the front.

Ron noticed one child trying to make a call on his cell phone and he playfully took it away from him. The child kept saying he had to call his father to come get him. Ron threw the phone to Sylvia who pretended to make a call herself while trying to see what calls or texts had been made on the phone. Then she threw it to Barry. A text in Russian shown clearly and Barry gave the phone to Kevin. Kevin dialed the number. The answer came in Russian. He replied in Russian and carried on a conversation for a few minutes.

"What did they say?"

"They asked the Dwarf if the bus had left the Compound yet."

Barry also wanted to know what the text said and Kevin told him that it said to call in when the bus left so they could intercept. Kevin also signaled to Ron to take the Dwarf child into custody.

Ron handcuffed him to the arm of the bus seat. He also pulled the mask off and found a child with a goatee and moustache.

Surprisingly the rest of the route went without interruption. At the airport the bus pulled up to the Finish Military plane. The Special Agents removed their costumes, leaving them in regular clothes with bulletproof vests. They went quickly from the bus onto the plane. Bulswiki gave them no trouble and held Sylvia's hand when they boarded.

And they were off to London and a flight on a United States Government plane to Washington, DC. After turning Bulswiki over to the Feds, the Special Agents returned to their home bases and on to other assignments.

CHAPTER SEVENTEEN

Word reached Indiana that Alexandria Bulswiki had been caught, returned, and incarcerated in Washington, DC. Charles Ko was still on the loose along with who knows how many of his operatives. The hunting game was still on. The problem in Indiana was that Andy and Abby were the game still being hunted.

Andy, always the one who injected humor into serious situations, said to the group brainstorming their current situation, "What was that old joke? She said she was game so I shot her." Groans all around.

"Where is Henny Youngman when we need him?"

"Andy, this is serious and no time for levity," scolded Abby.

Andy said, "How many times have I heard that?"

"A zillion, I suspect," said Alice. "Let's get back to business."

The Bulswiki news was good, but it didn't alleviate the problems faced in Woodfield or in Stoney Lonesome. Their instructions were to stay put, remain vigilant and wait for further instructions. So that's what they were doing in both venues.

The head count in Purity Manor II included Kat Hastings, pretending to be a new tenant leasing the property from one Abigail Abbott for the Fall season. They had long since stopped having her pretending to be Abigail Abbott. First of all, she didn't look a thing like Abby who was tall and thin while Kat was short and stocky.

Maggie Muldoon, the cook/housekeeper was going about her business as usual. That meant she was driving herself to the grocery and to Church on Sundays. John Wayne Wong, the houseboy and foster son of the Abbotts, was going to and from Bloomington to classes at Indiana University. Jason Riffey, the CIA agent, was there to protect the people in Stoney Lonesome and maybe even catch some intruders. Then there was Hilda and BJ Hanson, evidently permanent houseguests. There seemed to be some comfort in a crowd.

Kat and Jason didn't exactly hit it off when they first met. Jason was quiet, reserved, and all business. Kat was not. She could never quite loosen the shell covering him. Either she did not come across funny and cheerful to Jason or his outer covering was so thick it couldn't be penetrated, or he had absolutely no sense of humor at all. But that didn't stop Kat from trying. Determination was one of several of her finer characteristics.

Sheriff Simpson had not yet been apprised of the situation with the Abbotts when he stopped by to see what had transpired with the mysterious death of the Asian. He arrived in his old Ford truck with no markings of being an official. Approaching the front door, Jason stopped him at gunpoint. Abe was asked to show his credentials which he did reluctantly. Kat and Wong came running in saying that Abe was the country sheriff and a friend. Abe was admitted into the living room. Mad as a wet hen, Kat described him to Abby later, he wanted to know what dang thing was going on.

Jason wasn't sure what or how much to say. He called Rick before answering. Rick asked to talk to the Sheriff and when Abe was on the phone, Rick asked him to stay at Purity Manor until he got there. He left Woodfield right away leaving Andy and Abby without protection. They were to remain in Alice's apartment and if they were missing dinner, they were to order their meals delivered.

Rick arrived after Abe's feathers had been smoothed a bit, mostly by Maggie's brownies and cups of her special tea. He apologized for not bringing Abe into the loop, but both he and Jason were being ordered by the Pentagon and their CIA home offices to keep the information as quiet as possible. Everyone was afraid the press would get wind of it and splash it all over the media outlets.

Both Rick and Jason showed Abe their credentials and Abe seemed pleased to work with them. Rick then brought Abe up to date on the situation starting with the kidnapping and misinformation of Andy Abbott's purported death. He didn't leave anything out including the Alexandria Bulswiki and Charles Ko connection. He showed Abe their pictures that Rick had on his phone. Then he sent them to Abe's phone. He studied them carefully.

Rick didn't leave out Kat's connection to the Abbott's and to the failed attempt to kidnap Abby. That was the reason Kat got involved.

Rick even told Abe about the halfway successful invasion of the infamous Island and the capture of the barrels of venom but not the mad scientist. How the federal agents finally captured him in Russia and sneaked him out of Russia to Finland to England to the USA and incarceration.

And last he told him about Charles Ko, the Taiwan Industrialist, still on the loose and still trying to find Andy Abbott to kill him or kidnap Abby Abbott and trade her for Andy. He purposely did not tell Abe where he was keeping them protected. Best Abe didn't know for any number of reasons.

Everybody up to date now, they parted company and vowed to keep each other informed from now on. Jason apologized to Abe who slapped him on the back and told him he would have done the same given the same circumstances.

Rick went back to Woodfield and reported what all happened in Brown County. He mentioned to Abby that he noted that Kat and Jason were holding hands.

"I thought they didn't like each other," said Abby.

"Obviously they have come to some kind of infatuation."

"Infatuation?"

"Holding hands doesn't mean infatuation. It could just mean friendship," Abby declared.

"Or protection. Maybe Jason gets touchy-feely."

"Andy!"

"I'm just saying," laughed Andy.

Abe Simpson went about his day just like he always did. Only difference was that he was scrutinizing every stranger he met. Rick's description and information impressed him more than he would like to admit. Strangers could be on the bad guy side or they could be in town to shop.

Federal agents. Sounded like many units of the Government were involved in this man hunt. Chances were very slim that this Ko guy would be caught in Brown County and by a county sheriff at that. But you never know. So…. Abe was vigilant.

Several days passed and Abe began to relax a little while he was on duty. He chose not to tell his wife or his staff about the situation. The more people who knew, the more likely it would be that someone with a slip of the tongue would bring the press down upon them. That's all they needed. More traffic. But it would also scare off any chance of apprehending the guy with the white hair.

On the second Monday after Rick came to inform the Sheriff about Andy and Abby, Abe and his wife were eating in the hotel restaurant in Nashville. There were two men eating alone at one of the tables. Abe's wife casually said that those two men must not live here because they are by themselves, and no one is speaking to them. She also said sarcastically that one of the men had a bad hair job. Probably had some work done, too.

Abe, whose back was to them, dropped his napkin and bent over to pick it up. Neither man had white hair so he dismissed them. He was accustomed to his wife being critical of people. She was no beauty herself, but that didn't deter her from commenting on other people's appearance, fashion knowledge, or behavior. They had been married since they got out of High School. Long ago they had accepted each other's idiosyncrasies.

When the taller of the two men stood up to pay the bill at the cash register, Abe saw his resemblance to the white-haired man. This man had a lot of black hair and it looked strangely like patten leather. What could he do to detain this man? He didn't want to scare him off so he let him leave without alarming him. But he followed him to the Inn in the Brown County State Park. He stayed in the Parking Lot with a view of the front doors. If he left before morning, Abe would follow.

Abe called Rick who called Jason and they met Abe in the parking lot. They formulated a plan. Abe also called for his two deputies to meet him there. A squad of five lawmen were there to take Ko into custody when he emerged the following morning. Those odds were not very good if Ko had an army of killers with him. It would be what it would be. There was nothing to do but wait through the night.

In the meantime, Rick called his Bureau Chief who called his boss at the Pentagon and wheels were turning on both coasts but the engine was in Nashville, Indiana. Rick could only imagine the excitement of planes trying to land at Bloomington airport. He hoped no one called the Indianapolis branch of the FBI. They hadn't even let the Bloomington FBI know. Just in case.

Rick stationed Abe's two Deputies behind a bush on either side of the entrance walkway at the Front Doors. Rick and Jason hid behind parked cars also on either side of the entrance. Abe was the front man because he was the only one who could legally arrest anyone. The CIA couldn't. There was no FBI there. And no one from the DOD had arrived yet.

Dawn hadn't broken yet when Charles Ko came out the door carrying his luggage. Abe approached him while his Deputy stopped his companion before he could come to his boss' aid.

Showing his Sheriff's badge, he said in his usual drawl, Charles Ko, you are under arrest."

"My name isn't Charles Ko. And what am I under arrest for? I am merely a visitor enjoying the sights and sounds of Brown County in the Fall."

Hedging, Abe said, "We will have to go down to the jail and sort this out. We have an Arrest Warrant from the Federal Government to apprehend you and take you into custody."

By this time Rick and Jason had approached with guns drawn. The two Deputies had the other man handcuffed and on his knees. They went back inside and waited for the Paddy Wagon to come take everybody away. Only the Paddy Wagon never arrived. Instead it was blown up entering the Park. Everybody, including a State Policeman who was vacationing there, held vigil. Someone, a civilian, posted himself up the road from the entrance of the Inn parking lot. He was to tell them if someone was coming toward the Inn.

No one was allowed out and no one was let in.

National and international security agencies were all hunting for Charles Ko and he was captured by a County Sheriff in Nashville, Indiana. Indiana, it is said, is a state people only fly over. HA!

CHAPTER EIGHTEEN

The Feds did arrive and take Charles Ko into custody. His luggage and briefcase were apprehended and thoroughly searched. Several passports in different names were found. Took a while to sort out Ko's real name and occupation. It was done through DNA, fingerprints, and criminal records.

Turned out he was a former Chinese diplomat and a former inmate of a notorious Chinese prison. He was from a former Chinese Ruling family who was deposed in a riotous takeover. Most of them got out of China, but Ko was captured and jailed by the new regime as a dangerous dissident. With help from his family who had found refuge in Russia, he escaped the unescapable prison. Later he was apprehended by Chinese authorities and thought was killed, cremated, and his ashes given to his family and buried in the family crypt.

He was switched with an unclaimed body, nursed back to health, and sent out to rule the world by his very wealthy family.

He was Chinese on his father's side and English on his mother's which accounted for his tall stature and whiter skin. Authorities were running into all sorts of barriers trying to unearth the urn that supposedly contained his ashes.

Since he was listed and acknowledged as deceased, he was free to roam the world using any passport he had in his possession. Possibly because of torture in the Chinese prison, his brain was affected because he began to act irrationally. Or perhaps his irrational behavior was just an act. He and his former Chinese ruling family planned to regain their high position in China. He engaged the famously egotistical Scientist, Alexandria Bulswiki, to come up with a germ that could wipe out much of the world. Ko didn't realize by killing off so many people there would be less people to rule. Even less if he himself and many of his family members died of the plague. Obviously, logic didn't enter into his thinking.

Ko and Bulswiki were incarcerated in different places while being interrogated in Washington, DC. They never got in touch with each other. If so, it was never detected. They received no visitors other than their lawyers and interrogators. They both had several well-known attorneys. Unfortunately – or maybe fortunately – none of the lawyers were background-checked before allowed to talk privately with their clients. Since they were all citizens of the United States and members of the American Bar Association, it was assumed they were above suspect. Considering what happened later, at least one should have been suspected. Or maybe it was two.

Many reporters and TV news people came to ask Abe Simpson what had gone on in Nashville when so many branches of government had descended on the small Indiana community. Abe had been told, supposedly by the President of The United States, to tell reporters that it was a false alarm. It was originally thought that a kidnapped child on the "Most Wanted List" had been found in Indiana. That was not the case. The child in question, reported by a viewer of the popular TV show, was not kidnapped. He was camping with his family in the State Park and was seen in the local grocery store. There was a slight resemblance, but Abe got it all straightened out and the media people left to pursue other more interesting news.

After things calmed down in Nashville, Rick took Andy and Abby back to Stoney Lonesome. While still being cautious, they encountered nothing suspicious. Rick thought there was a very good chance that Ko still had people hunting for Andy, and perhaps Abby, with orders to kill them on sight. Nothing suspicious had happened in over a month. Still, he kept them protected. And Jason did the same in Purity Manor.

On their very first visit, Andy was greeted by the faithful Maggie Muldoone. Wong had already seen him many times at Woodfield. Pamfou jumped up and down excitedly and never left his side inside the house or outside the compound.

Andy was very impressed with what was now his new second home. Abby showed him all around the house. She even showed him around the property with Rick and Jason both trailing behind. They stopped by the place where his Japanese messenger, Naka, was shot by, Rick thought, Oliver Gutinov. That case was never solved and probably wouldn't be now. Ollie had somehow disappeared and hadn't been heard from or seen since the night he was pulled into the black limousine by Mr. Ko.

Andy and Abby had discussed returning to the West Coast after this episode in their lives ended. They couldn't continue with their careers like nothing happened. Something had happened. Andy was reported dead in a plane crash and was eulogized by the film industry, friends, and co-workers. BOLD headlines read: PRODUCER KILLED IN PLANE CRASH. That was big news in Hollywood. His widow had sold their Bel Air home and moved to New Mexico, presumably retired from the business. They couldn't suddenly appear with no explanation of what had happened.

"I can't mimic Mark Twain and say, 'Reports of my death has been greatly exaggerated' and get away with it." Andy laughed, but he knew he couldn't tell people what really happened. The government wouldn't allow it.

"We can't say that you were away at a Spa getting work done to make you look younger," kidded Abby.

"Are you saying I do look older?" Andy slumped to appear old.

"Of course not. You look like Cary Grant, Cary.

"Why not say you were kidnapped and held hostage for ransom. You escaped and followed Abigail's trail from New Mexico to Indiana. Case closed."

"Reporters aren't going to settle for that," Abby argued.

"You're a writer. Make up answers on the spot."

"Yes," Rick. "I can do that."

Rick reminded them that even though they return to Los Angeles and their careers, they still have to appear in court during the promised over-long trials. Until that time, they would have to have security. "Who knows how influential Ko's Chinese family continues to be."

"I thought word of their plans to return to leadership in China was passed along to the current leaders there," said Andy.

"That is true. And we hope they take care of that family of adversaries themselves. But when will we find out if they did?"

"Rick, we probably won't ever know for certain. In the meantime, we are going to continue with our lives. We have already wasted almost three years. We have a script about ready to produce and we will work hard to achieve that end. Writing, Producing, and Directing is our lives. We are anxious to get back to it."

"Point taken. Just be aware and be careful." Rick knew it would take a long time, if ever, for both of the Abbotts to feel completely safe. They would live their lives being aware and suspicious day in and day out.

Kat and Jason, who had begun a relationship, were in no hurry to return to their lives back home. Since Kat was settled in St. Louis and Jason was retired on his Iowa farm, they had not decided where to continue their lives together. Jason liked the shore and Kat liked the desert, discussion was about Phoenix and San Diego. Abby, when told about the romance, suggested a halfway solution in Palm Desert or Palm Springs. Either place would be near her and Andy in Los Angeles. It was finally decided that Kat didn't like the desert as much as Jason liked the shore so it was agreed they would settle in Escondido, California. They began looking for property online in and around Escondido. Rick began looking for property in the LA area for Andy and Abby. He didn't want Andy or Abby listed on anything like a Deed that could be traced. Abby suggested they go to the Bridwell Agency that sold her the Stoney Lonesome property. Rick vetoed that suggestion. Too many details might be innocently asked and told.

"For now, let's not do anything that might jeopardize the government's case against both Ko and Bulswiki," said Rick. "We have been safe so far by being patient."

It wasn't very long before news came that both Ko and Bulswiki took their own lives by biting on cyanide capsules. Odd that both decided to do away with themselves at the same time with the same kind of poison pill that no one knows how they obtained. They must have had help? Duh!

Ko's family tried to claim both bodies, but the government wanted to dissect both of their brains. Through some legal maneuvering they got permission, and it was presumed that their studies showed something of value in the study of the human mind. Of course, no information came to light. Someday information gathered from those demented brains might be helpful in cures or at least the understanding of behavior patterns.

Miraculously, the media only got word that one prisoner in two different prisons, completely unrelated to each other, died of natural causes. The media was busy reporting on the political debates of the candidates running for the presidency and the severe weather across the nation. That news in itself was alarming. And dangerous. Never mind the near miss germ warfare.

Finally it was time to get back to their normal lives, if normal ever described any of their lives. The last evening they were at Woodfield they had a Pizza Party in Alice's apartment. Rick ordered in Pizza from Mama Bear's Pizza for Alice's posse. He thanked Maysie, Ione, and Joyce for their help in keeping Cary safe. He also explained that Cary would be safe now that his enemies were dead and the case was closed. He tried to explain that Cary was really Andrew Abbott, the Hollywood producer and husband of Abigail Abbott, without giving any details of the truth. He told them that Andy had been kidnapped for ransom and reported killed in an attempted escape. He showed up here hunting Abby and was hidden in Alice's apartment. They knew the rest of the story.

It was a happy ending to an exciting time in Woodfield. They all agreed that Cary would be missed and they made him promise to invite them to the opening of his next Motion Picture no matter where it was shown. He promised to do that. As an afterthought, he said his next picture's opening night would take place in Bloomington at Woodfield. They would all be the Guests of Honor.

"I hope I live that long," said Mayzie.

"Mayzie!' scolded Joyce.

"I'm just saying. Nothing is certain. I always wear clean underwear when I go on the Shopping Bus. Just in case."

Everyone laughed. Mayzie always kept everybody laughing.

Ione added, "Mayzie always said she wanted to go out laughing."

The evening ended with hugs all around.

Rick, Andy, and Abigail flew out to California together and parted ways at LAX.

Rick said, "This is a story that will never be told."

"Don't bet on it," said Andy.

THE END